CART &
CWIDDER

CART &
CWIDDER

DIANA WYNNE JONES

Collier Books
Macmillan Publishing Company
New York

First Collier Books edition 1990

Collier Books
Macmillan Publishing Company
866 Third Avenue, New York, NY 10022

Printed in the United States of America

10 9 8 7 6 5 4 3 2 1

              Library of Congress Cataloging-in-Publication Data
Jones, Diana Wynne.
    Cart & cwidder/Diana Wynne Jones.
      p.   cm.
    Originally published: New York: Atheneum, 1977.
    Summary: When their father, a traveling minstrel, is killed, three children involved
in rebellion and intrigue inherit a lutelike cwidder with more than musical powers.
    ISBN 0-02-043921-0
    [1. Fantasy.] I. Title. II. Title: Cart and cwidder.
PZ7.J684Car 1990
[Fic]—dc20   89-25395 CIP AC

FOR RACHEL

CART &
CWIDDER

Chapter I

"Do come out of that dream, Moril," Lenina said.

"Glad-rags, Moril," said Brid. "We're nearly in Derent."

Moril sighed reproachfully. He had not been in a dream, and he felt it was unfair of his mother to call it that. He had merely been gazing at the white road as it wandered northwards, thinking how glad he was to be going that way again, and how glad he would be to get out of the South. It was spring, and it was already far too hot. But that was not the worst of the South. The worst, to Moril's mind, was the need to be careful. You dared not put a foot, or a word, out of place for fear of being clapped in jail. People were watching all the time to report what you said. It gave Moril the creeps. And it irked him that there were songs his father dared not sing in the South for fear of sounding seditious. They were the best songs, too, to Moril's mind. They all came from the North. Moril himself had been born in the North, in the earldom of Hannart. And his favourite hero, the Adon, had once upon a time been Earl of Hannart.

"You're dreaming again!" Lenina said sharply.

"No, I'm not," said Moril. He left his perch behind the driving-seat and climbed hastily into the covered back of the cart. His mother and his

1

sister were already changed into their cheap tinsel-trimmed show dresses. Lenina, who was pale and blonde and still very beautiful, was in silver and pale gold. Brid, who was darker and browner, had a glimmering peacock dress. Lenina hung Moril's suit above the rack of musical instruments, and Moril squeezed up to that end to change, very careful not to bang a cwidder or scrape the hand-organ. Each instrument was shiny with use and gleaming with care. Each had its special place. Everything in the cart did. Clennen insisted on it. He said that life in a small cart would otherwise become impossible.

Once Moril was changed, he emerged from the cart as a very flamboyant figure, for his suit was the same peacock as Brid's dress and his hair was red—a bright wild red. He had inherited Lenina's paleness. His face was white, with a few red freckles.

"You know, Mother," Brid said, as she had said before every show since they left Holand, "I don't think I like that colour on Moril."

"It makes people notice him," said Lenina, and went to take the reins while Clennen and Dagner changed in their turn.

Moril went to walk in the damp springing grass on the roadside, that was rough-soft under his toes, where he could have a good view of the cart that was his home. It was painted in a number of noticeable colours, principally pink and gold. Picked out in gold and sky-blue along the sides were the words: *CLENNEN THE SINGER*. Moril knew it was garish, but he loved this cart all the same. It moved softly, because it was well-sprung and well-oiled, and ran easily behind Olob, the glistening brown horse. Clennen always said he would not part with Olob for an earldom. Olob—his real name was Barangarolob, because Clennen loved long names—was harnessed in pink and scarlet, with a great deal of polished brass, and looked as magnificent as the rest of the turnout. Moril was just thinking that his mother and Brid on the driving-seat looked like two queens—or perhaps a queen and a princess—when Clennen stuck his head out of the canvas at the back.

"Admiring us, are you?" he called cheerfully. Moril smiled and nodded. "It's like life," Clennen said. "You may wonder what goes on inside, but what matters is the look of it and the kind of performance we give. Remember that." His head popped back inside again.

Moril went on smiling. His father was always giving them odd thoughts to remember. He would probably want this one repeated to him in a day or so. Moril thought about it—in the dreamy way in which he usually gave his attention to anything— and he could not see that their turnout was like life. Life was not pink and gold. At least, some of theirs was, he supposed, but that was only saying the cart *was* life.

He was still pondering, when they came under some big trees covered with pale buds, and the canvas cover went down with a bit of a clatter, revealing Clennen and Dagner dressed in scarlet and ready for the show. Moril scampered back and climbed up with them. Clennen smiled jovially. Dagner, whose face was tight and pinched, as it always was before a show, pushed Moril's cwidder into his hands and Moril into the right place without a word. He handed the big old cwidder to Clennen and the panhorn to Brid, and took up a pipe and a long thin drum himself. By the time they were all settled, Olob was clopping smoothly into the main square of Derent.

"Ready," said Clennen. "Two, three." And they struck up.

Derent was not a big place. The number of people who came into the square in response to their opening song was not encouraging. There was a trickle of children and ten adults at the most. True, the people sitting outside the tavern turned their chairs round to get a better view, but Moril had a vague feeling, all the same, that they were wasting their talents on Derent. He said so to Brid, while Lenina was reaching past him to receive the hand-organ from Dagner.

"All your feelings are vague!" Lenina said, overhearing. "Be quiet."

Undaunted by the sparse crowd, Clennen began his usual patter. "Ladies and gentlemen, come and listen! I am Clennen the Singer, on my way from Holand to the North. I bring you news, views, songs and tales, things old and things new. Roll up, draw up chairs, come near and listen!" Clennen had a fine rolling voice, speaking or singing. It rumbled round the square. Eyes were drawn to him, for his presence matched his voice. He was a big man, and not a thin one, though the scarlet suit made his paunch look bigger than it really was. He had a good sharp curl of ginger beard, which made up for the bald patch at the back of his head—now hidden by his scarlet hat. But the main thing about him was his enormous, jovial, total good humour.

It seemed to fetch people by magic, or multiply those there out of thin air. Before his speech was over, there were forty or fifty people listening to it.

"So there!" Brid said to Moril.

Before the performance could start, however, someone pushed up to the cart, calling: "Have you got any news from Holand, Clennen?" So they had to wait. They were used to this. Moril thought of it as part of the performance—and it certainly seemed to be one of their duties—to bring news from one part of Dalemark to the others. In the South particularly, there were few other ways in which people could get to know what was happening in the next lordship, let alone the next earldom.

"Now, let's see," said Clennen. "There's been a new earl invested for the South Dales—the old one's grandson. And they tell me Hadd has fallen out with Henda again." This surprised nobody. They were two very quarrelsome earls. "And I *hear*," said Clennen, stressing the *hear*, to show that he was not trying to stir up trouble, "I *hear* the cause of it had something to do with a shipload of Northmen that came into harbour at Holand last month." This caused confused and careful muttering. Nobody knew what to make of a ship from the North coming into Holand, or whether they were breaking the law to think of it at all. Clennen passed on to other news. "The Earl of Waywold is making new money—copper and goodness knows what else in it—worth nothing. You get more than two thousand to one gold. Now the price on the Porter—you've all heard of the Porter, I suppose?" Everyone had. The Porter was a notorious spy, much wanted by the earls of the South for passing illegal information

5

and stirring up discontent. Not one of the earls had been able to catch him. "The price on the Porter's head now being two thousand gold," said Clennen, "it's to be hoped that he's not taken in Waywold, or you'll have to collect your reward in a waggon." This caused some cautious laughter. "And the storm last month carried off the lord's roof in Bradbrook, not to speak of my tent," said Clennen.

Lenina, by this time, had sorted out the strips of paper on which she had written messages from people in other places to friends and relatives in Derent. She began calling them out. "Is there someone called Coran here? I've a message from his uncle at Pennet." A red-faced young man pushed forward. He confessed, as if he were ashamed of it, that he could read, and was handed the paper. "Is there a Granny Ben here?"

"She's sick, but I'll tell her," someone called.

So it went on. Lenina handed out messages to those who could read, and read them out to those who could not. More people hurried into the square, hearing there was news. Shortly, there was a fair throng of people, all in great good humour, all telling one another the latest news from Holand.

Then Clennen called out: "Now I'm putting my hat on the ground here. If you want a song of us too, do us the favour of filling it with silver." The scarlet hat spun neatly on to the cobblestones and waited, looking empty and expectant. Clennen waited too, with rather the same look. And after a second, the red-faced Coran, grateful for his message, tossed a silver coin into it. Another followed, and another. Lenina, watching expertly, muttered to Brid that it looked like good takings.

After that, the performance began in earnest. Moril did not have much time even for vague thinking. Though he did not do much of the singing, his job was to play treble to the low sweet notes of his father's big cwidder, and he was kept fairly busy. His fingers grew hot and tingly, and he leant over and blew on them to cool them as he played. Clennen, as he had promised the crowd, gave them old favourites and new favourites—ballads, love-songs and comic songs—and some songs that were entirely new. Several of these were his own. Clennen was a great maker of songs. Brid and Dagner joined him for some of them, or played panhorn, drum and third cwidder, and Lenina played stolidly on the hand-organ. She played well—since Clennen had taught her—but always rather mechanically, as if her mind were elsewhere. And Moril fingered away busily, his left hand sliding up and down the long, inlaid arm of his cwidder, his right thrumming on the strings until his fingertips glowed.

Every so often, Clennen would pause and send a cheerfully reproachful look towards his hat. This usually caused a hand to come out from the crowd and drop a small, shamed coin in with the others. Then Clennen would beam round at everyone and go on again. When the hat was more than half full, he said: "Now I think the time has come for some of the songs out of our past. As you may know, the history of Dalemark is full of fine singers, but, to my mind, there have never been two to compare with the Adon and Osfameron. Neither has ever been equalled. But Osfameron was an ancestor of mine. I happen to be descended from him in a direct line, father to son. And it was said of Osfameron that he

7

could charm the rocks from the mountains, the dead from their sleep, and the gold from men's purses." Here, a slight raising of Clennen's sandy eyebrows in the direction of the hat called forth an apologetic penny and a ripple of laughter from everyone. "So, ladies and gentlemen," said Clennen, "I shall now sing four songs by Osfameron."

Moril sighed and leant his cwidder carefully against the side of the cart. The old songs only needed the big cwidder, so he could have a rest. In spite of this, he wished his father would not sing them. Moril much preferred the new, full-bodied music. The old required a fingering which made even the big mellow cwidder sound cracked and thin, and Clennen seemed to find it necessary to change his deep singing voice until it became thin, high and peculiar. As for the words—Moril listened to the first song and wondered what Osfameron had been on about.

> *The Adon's hall was open. Through it*
> *Swallows darted. The soul flies through life.*
> *Osfameron in his mind's eye knew it.*
> *The bird's life is not the man's life.*

But the crowd appreciated it. Moril heard someone say: "I do like to hear the old songs done in the right way." And when they were over, there was a round of applause and a few more coins.

Then Dagner, with his face more tight and pinched than ever, took up his cwidder. Clennen said: "I now introduce my eldest son, Dastgandlen Handagner." This was Dagner's full name. Clennen loved long names. "He will sing you some of his own songs." said Clennen, and waved Dagner forward into the centre of the cart. Dagner, with a grimace of pure nervousness, bowed to the crowd and began to sing. Moril could never understand why this part was such a torment to Dagner. He knew his brother would have died rather than missed his part in the performance, yet he was never happy until it was over. Perhaps it was because Dagner had made the songs himself.

They were strange, moody little songs, with odd rhythms. Dagner made them even odder, by singing now loud, now soft, for no real reason, unless it was nerves. And they had a haunting something. The tunes stuck in your head and you hummed them when you thought you had long forgotten them. Moril listened and watched, and envied Dagner this gift of making songs. He would have given—well—his toes, anyway, to be able to compose anything.

> *The colour in your head*
> *The colour in your mind*
> *Is dead*
> *If you follow it blind,*

Dagner sang, and the crowd grew to like it. Dagner was not remarkable to look at—he was thin and sandy-haired, with a large Adam's apple—and people expected his songs to be unremarkable too. But when he finished, there was applause and some more coins. Dagner flushed pale purple with pleasure and was almost at ease for the rest of the show.

There was not much more. The whole family sang a few more songs together and wound up with *Jolly Holanders*. They always finished with that in the South, and the audience always joined in. Then

9

it was a matter of putting away the instruments and replying to the things people came up to say.

This was always rather a confused time. There were the usual number of people who seemed to know Clennen well; the usual giggly girls who wanted Dagner to tell them how he composed songs—a thing Dagner could never explain and always tried to do; the usual kind people who told Moril he was quite a musician for a youngster; and the usual gentlemen who drifted up to Lenina and Brid and tried to murmur sweet nothings to them. Clennen was always very quick to notice these gentlemen, particularly those who approached Brid. Poor Brid looked older than she was in her show-clothes—she was really only just thirteen—and she did not know how to deal with murmuring gentlemen at all.

"Well, you see, my father taught me," Moril explained.

"They come into my head like—er—ideas," Dagner explained.

"It is Lenina, isn't it?" murmured a gentleman at the head of the cart.

"It is," said Lenina.

"I didn't quite hear what you said," Brid said rather desperately to another gentleman.

"I don't go to Hannart. I had a little disagreement with the Earl," said Clennen. He swung round and, with one comprehensive look, disposed of the man Brid could not hear and also the one who thought Lenina was herself. "But I'm going through Dropwater and beyond," he continued, turning back to his friends.

Lenina had collected the money and was counting

it. "Good," she said. "We can stay at the inn here. I fancy a roof over my head."

Moril and Brid fancied it too. It was the height of luxury. There would be feather beds, a proper bath, and real food cooked indoors. Brid licked her lips and gave Moril a delighted grin. Moril smiled back in his milky, sleepy way.

"No. No time," said Clennen, when at last he was free to be asked. "We have to press on. We're picking up a passenger on the road."

Lenina said nothing. It was not her way. While Brid, Moril and even Dagner protested, she simply picked up the reins and encouraged Olob to move.

Chapter II

"Where are we picking up the passenger?" Brid enquired when they were three miles or so beyond Derent and her discontent had worn off somewhat. She was back in her everyday blue check and looked rather younger than she was.

"Couple of miles on. I'll tell you where," Clennen said to Dagner, who was driving.

"Going North, is he?" Dagner said.

"That's right," said Clennen.

Moril, in the ordinary rust-coloured clothes he preferred, and in which, to Brid's mind, he looked a great deal nicer, trotted along beside the cart and hoped vaguely that the passenger would be agreeable. They had taken a woman last year who had driven him nearly crazy with boredom. She had known a hundred little boys, and they were all better than Moril in some way, and she had at least two long stories about each boy to prove it. They took someone most years, going North. Since North and South had begun their long disagreement, very little traffic went between. Those who had no horse—and to walk meant the risk of being taken up as a vagrant and clapped into jail—had to rely on such people as the licensed singers to take them as paying passengers.

12

The disagreement had begun so far in the past that not many people knew its cause: the North had one version, the South another. But it was certain that three kings of Dalemark had died, one after another, without leaving a proper heir to the throne. And almost every earl in the land had some kind of claim to be king. Even before the last king took the kingstone and ruled from Hannart in the North, there had been quarrels and wars, and the country showed signs of breaking up into its separate earldoms. And when the Adon, who was the last king, died, his heirs were not to be found and neither was the kingstone. Civil war began in earnest.

Since then, the only rulers of Dalemark had been the earls, each in his own earldom, with the lords under them. At first, the earls of the South had grouped together simply to stop the earls of Hannart from becoming kings. And when the ordinary people in the South showed signs of wanting a king from Hannart, those who dared say so were hanged. The earls of the North, who were a more independent lot, became indignant at this and slowly grouped in support of Hannart. Times changed. No one now wanted a king. Keril, the present Earl of Hannart, said publicly that he had no claim to the throne. But the disagreement ran deeper than ever. The men of the North claimed that half the land was enslaved, and the earls of the South said the North was plotting against them. The year Brid was born, Keril, Earl of Hannart, had been proclaimed a public enemy by every earl and lord in the South. After that, the only people who dared travel between were accredited traders and licensed singers, and they had to prove that their business was harmless or they might be arrested anywhere in the South.

Moril had met some of the traders and quite a few of the singers. Clennen did not speak highly of any of them, except perhaps the singer Hestefan, whom Moril had not met. But Moril had never heard any of them complain of having to take passengers. He thought they must all be very patient people.

"What about payment?" asked Lenina.

"You wait and see," said Clennen, with a laugh.

"That's all very well," said Brid, returning to her discontent. "But why do we always have to take someone? Why can't the stupid North make friends with the silly South?"

"You tell me," said Clennen. And, after Brid had stammered for a minute, he laughed and said, "Would *you* make friends with someone you knew would stab you in the back if he got the chance? Remember that. Mind you, there was a time when the South was as free a place as the North. Remember that too."

This was a bold thing to say in the South. The last rebellion had been stamped out very harshly indeed, and the strict laws were still in force. You did not say anything that suggested you were discontented with the ways of the South.

That had been the latest of a whole series of uprisings. The first few had been in North and South alike, and those had all been led by people claiming to be the lost kings. The earls of the North had taken them lightly. Since the mountains in the North always made rebels and criminals hard to catch, the laws of Hannart and of Gardale had long forbidden things like taking the families of rebels as hostages or laying waste their homes. So the earls fought the rebels, parleyed with them and sometimes joined them. Whatever their reasons, Clennen was fond of saying, "The earls of the North treated their enemies like men."

It was different in the lowlands of the South. There were no hiding places and no customs of mercy. The earls stamped out the false kings hard and bloodily, and went on to slaughter the families of their followers. Then they got together to impose new laws and terrible penalties for anyone who rebelled again. And what happened was that rebellion died out in the North, but discontent and uprisings went on and on in the South. The laws became ever more severe. And this had its effect on the earls there. They became accustomed to having the power of life and death over their subjects and were scornful of the weak ways of the North. Yet they were also extremely frightened of what the ordinary people might do to them, should an uprising be successful. So they made more and fiercer laws.

The result was that many people fled from the South to the North. There they plotted further rebellion—or were feared by the earls of the South to be doing so. The earls demanded that the North either send these people back or put them to death. The earls of the North came together and replied, in a letter, which Clennen had made all his children learn by heart. It was, he said, a famous piece of History. "What goes on in a man's head," the earls of the North said, "is his own business. We do not hang him because he thinks he has a grievance. Nor, according to the laws of Hannart, do we hand him over to another man to hang." That had been over fifty years ago, but, as Clennen said, it was still the same today. And it showed the importance of Hannart. For, no matter what the disagreement, whether over kings or common men, Hannart had always been at the heart of it. Keril, the present Earl of Hannart, had helped to organize the last uprising and spoken out against the South ever since. The earls of the South hated and feared all the North, but Hannart most of all. The country-side was known to be full of spies and informers, watching and listening to give warning of rebellious thoughts.

That was why, when Clennen spoke of North, South and freedom in the same breath, Moril saw Lenina look round the hedges to make sure no one was listening. He found himself doing the same.

But the hedges, though the leaves were already dusty, were still thin enough to see through. Nothing moved in them but birds. The only people they saw, for the next mile or so, were in the distance, planting vines on a hillside, until they came to where a road branched off to another vineyard. There, on the triangle made by the turning, a man was waiting. At his feet he had a huge round bottle half encased in a straw basket. He waved and Dagner drew up. Olob turned his head and looked at the huge bottle with evident misgiving.

"Evening, Flind," said Clennen. "Is that our payment there by your feet?" The man nodded. He seemed disinclined to smile, though Clennen smiled broadly at him. "I hoped it was," said Clennen. "Where's the passenger?"

Flind jerked a thumb. The passenger, probably in an attempt to keep out of the sun, was sitting behind the bottle in its shadow. He looked very hot, very untidy, rather discontented, and rather younger than Dagner.

"Help him into the cart," Clennen said to Moril.

Moril did his best, but the passenger shook off his helping hand. "I can get in by myself," he said, "I'm not a cripple." He climbed in very nimbly and sat on the floor. The canvas cover was half up and he seemed glad of its shade. Moril looked vaguely after him and hoped it was the heat that made him feel so disagreeable. He knew from bitter experience that someone around Dagner's age could make life very unpleasant if he was steadily disagreeable for some hundreds of miles. This could be worse than the woman last year. He looked at Brid, who made her squeezed-lemon face back.

Clennen and Flind, meanwhile, were heaving the huge jar through the tailgate of the cart. It took a good deal of effort, and a lot of space once it was in. Olob almost laid his head backwards over his shoulders in an attempt to show his strong disapproval of it.

"Are you really taking our payment in wine?" said Lenina.

"Can you think of a better one?" said Clennen. "My dear girl, there's only beer to drink in the North! Count your blessings. We'll broach it this evening, shall we? Or would you rather wait until we're going through Markind?"

"Oh—this evening," said Lenina, smiling a little.

17

Clennen latched the tailgate, waved to Flind, and they went on. Olob made a very expressive business of getting the cart under way again. Brid was quite sorry for him, straining in front of all that extra weight, but everyone else knew that the cart was so well sprung and greased that Olob could hardly feel the difference. Dagner made no bones about flicking him with the whip.

"What a lazy horse!" exclaimed the passenger.

"They're often the wisest ones," said Clennen.

The passenger, realising he had been snubbed, put his chin on his knees and sighed gustily. Brid and Moril took turns at eyeing him through the gap in the tailgate. He was burlier than Dagner, though he was younger, and much the same height. But he was more remarkable-looking, because he was a queer combination of dark and fair. His hair was tawny-fair, and there was a lot of it, like a lion's mane only rather more untidy, and his eyes were a pale blue-green. But his eyebrows were thick and black and his skin very brown. His nose put them in mind of an eagle. He still had that fed-up look, which they decided must be due to more than the heat.

"Perhaps his grandfather's dying, and they sent for him, and he doesn't want to go," Brid speculated. Moril was content to leave it vague. He simply hoped the passenger would not vent his annoyance on them.

A mile or so further on, Clennen said: "We haven't got your name, lad. There's a lot in a name, I always think. What is it?"

"It's Kialan," said the passenger. "With a K."

"Even with a K, it's not half long enough for me," said Clennen.

"Well, what do you expect me to say? It's really my name!" the passenger protested.

"I like longer names," Clennen explained. "Clennen's too short for me too. Lenina—my wife's name—is too short. But my children all have good spreading names, because I could choose them myself. The lad driving is Dastgandlen Handagner, my daughter is Cennoreth Manaliabrid, and the one with the red hair is Osfameron Tanamoril."

Moril ground his teeth and waited for the passenger to laugh. But, in fact, he looked rather awed. "Oh," he said. "Er—do you call them all that when you want to speak to them?"

"And the lazy-wise horse is Barangarolob," Clennen added, perfectly seriously, as if he were simply anxious for Kialan to know. Dagner gave a little whinny of laughter, which might have come from Olob. Kialan looked piteous.

"Take no notice," said Lenina. "They're Dagner, Brid and Moril for short. And the horse is Olob."

Kialan looked relieved. He gave another gusty sigh or so and took off his coat. He must have been hot in it, because it was a thick coat, of good cloth. Brid whispered that it must be his best one, but Moril had lost interest in Kialan by then and did not care. Kialan folded the coat—not as carefully as such a good garment deserved—and used it as a pillow while he pretended to go to sleep. Brid knew he was only pretending, because he started up every time any travellers passed them and looked through the opening in the cover to see who they were.

There was not much traffic on the road. Mostly, it was slow waggons, which Olob trotted past without any difficulty, sending spurts of white grit from beneath the cartwheels, until Moril, trotting in the rear, seemed to have hair the same colour as Clennen's. But there were a few horsemen, and these overtook Olob as easily as Olob overtook the waggons. Once, quite a group of riders came past, raising a whirl of white dust, and were scanned by Kialan with great interest. One of the group seemed equally interested in them. He craned round in his saddle as he passed to get a good look at the cart.

"Who was that fellow?" Clennen said to Lenina.

"I couldn't say," she answered.

"Funny," said Clennen, "I seem to have seen him before." But, since the man was a perfectly neutral-looking person, neither dark nor fair and neither young nor old, Clennen could not place him and gave up the attempt.

Shortly after that, as the sun was getting low, Olob left the road of his own accord and jolted the cart among gorse bushes into a heathy meadow. He stopped near a stream.

"Olob thinks this'll do," Dagner said to Clennen. "Will it?"

"You don't really let your horse choose where to stop!" Kialan exclaimed.

"He doesn't often let us down," said Clennen, surveying the meadow. "Yes, very nice. Horses have a gift for stopping, Kialan. Remember that."

The fed-up look settled on Kialan's face and he watched, a little scornfully, while Dagner unharnessed Olob and led him off to drink. He watched Moril wiping the dust off the cart and Brid collecting firewood.

"Don't offer to help, will you?" Brid muttered in his direction.

While Lenina was cooking supper, Clennen fetched the big cwidder down, polished it, tuned it carefully, and beckoned Moril. Moril came reluctantly. He was rather in awe of the big cwidder. Its shining round belly was even more imposing than Clennen's. The inlaid patterns on the front and arm, made of pearl and ivory and various coloured woods, puzzled him by their strangeness. And its voice when you played it was so surprisingly sweet and quite unlike that of the other cwidders. Clennen took such care of it that Moril still sometimes thought—as he had when he was little—that this cwidder was an extra, special part of Clennen, more important than his father's arm or leg—something on the lines of a wooden soul.

"Let's have that song of Osfameron's," said Clennen.

Moril liked the old songs so little that he was making very heavy weather of learning them. Clennen corrected him, made him go back to the beginning, and twice stopped him in the middle of the second verse. To make matters worse, Kialan came over and stood himself in front of Moril, listening. Moril, in self-defence, went into a dream between two notes, and stopped. He was with the Adon, on a green road in the North.

"Do you really need to teach him?" said Kialan.

"How else," asked Clennen, "do you think he'd learn?"

Kialan seemed a bit confused. "Well—I sort of supposed they picked it up—from giving shows," he said.

"Or it grew naturally, along with hair and fingernails?" Clennen suggested.

"No—I—Oh, that's silly!" said Kialan and, to Moril's relief, he drifted away. But he drifted back when Moril had finished and Brid took his place. Kialan caught Moril's sleeve. "I say, you all know all this music, but I suppose you can't even read and write, can you?"

Moril removed his sleeve. "Of course I can," he said. "My mother taught us." Before Kialan could ask any more impertinent questions, he scurried off among the gorse bushes to the stream. He stayed there, lost in vagueness, watching the bright water hurry over the different brightness of the stones beneath, until he heard Brid shouting.

"Supper! *Wash*, Moril!"

Supper was not very good, and what little bread they had was stale. "I say, this tastes peculiar!" Kialan said, pushing his share about on his plate.

Lenina's face, which never had much expression, went quite blank. "I meant to buy bread and onions in Derent," she said. "But there was no time."

There was a heavy pause. Then Clennen said, "Look, lad, we've got to travel more than a hundred and fifty miles together, you and us. It needs a little give and take, don't you think? I'd hate to have to break a good cwidder over your head."

The sun was setting then and the light was red. But Moril thought that this did not entirely account for the colour of Kialan's face. Kialan, however, said nothing. He silently accepted some of the wine, and drank it, but he did not speak again until much later. By then, Clennen had become very jolly with the wine. Beaming in the firelight, he leant back against the wheel of the cart and said to Dagner, "Give us that new song of yours."

"It's not quite ready yet," said Dagner. But, since this was not a performance, he willingly fetched his cwidder and picked out a sketch of what Moril thought was a very promising tune. And, without a trace of nervousness, he half-sang, half-spoke the words.

> Come with me, come with me.
> The blackbird asks you, "Follow me."
> No one will know, no one will know,
> Wherever you go, I shall go.
> Come with me. Morning spreads,
> Clouds are high in milky threads,
> The moon looks like a white thumbnail,
> Larks are singing up the dale.
> The sun is up, so follow me.
> I'd like us to go secretly
> Along the road, across the hill
> Where water runs and woods are still.

"And then I think the first four lines again," Dagner said, looking up at Clennen.

"No," said Clennen. "Won't do."

"Well, I needn't have them again," Dagner said humbly.

"I mean the whole thing won't do," said Clennen.

Dagner looked very dashed. Kialan seemed unable to stop himself saying indignantly: "Why? I thought it was going to be a jolly good song."

"The tune's all right, as far as it's gone," said Clennen. "But why spoil a tune like that with those words?"

"They're jolly good words," Kialan insisted. "I liked them."

"It's the words I seem to want," Dagner said diffidently.

"I see," said Clennen. "Then in that case don't utter them again until we're in the North—unless you want us taken up for rebels."

Dagner tried to explain. "But I—it wasn't. I was just trying to say how much I liked travelling in the cart and—and so on."

"Were you?" said Clennen. "And haven't you heard the songs the freedom-fighters used to sing here the year of the rebellion—oh, it'll be sixteen years ago now, the year you were born? They never dared say a thing straight out, so it was all put sideways—*Follow the Lark* was one, *Free as air and secret* another went, and the best known was *Come up the dale with me.* The lords here still hang a man on the spot for singing words like that."

"And I do think that's ridiculous!" Kialan burst out. "Why can't people sing what they want here? What's the matter with everyone?"

Brid and Moril looked at his firelit face with interest. It began to seem as if Kialan might be a freedom-fighter. They felt they could forgive him much if he was. Clennen, however, simply seemed amused.

"I hope there's not someone behind the gorse listening to you," he said. Kialan's head jerked round towards the nearest looming bush. "See?" said Clennen. "That's why, in one easy lesson, lad.

24

No one can trust anyone any more. It comes of uneasy rulers paying uneasy men to make the rest uneasy too. It's not always been like that, you know. Dagner, what did I say outside Derent?"

Dagner's mind was woefully on his unsuitable song. "Oh—er—something about life being only a performance, I think."

"I knew I could trust you to get the wrong saying—and the wrong saying wrong," Clennen said tolerantly. "Anyone?"

"You said the South was once as free as the North," said Brid. "You said it to me, really."

"Then remember it," said Clennen.

Chapter III

After one night attempting to share the smaller tent with Kialan and Dagner, Moril took to creeping into the cart along with Brid and the winejar. As he told Brid, even the winejar took up less space than Kialan, and it did not have knees and elbows. Moril had woken up three times to find himself out among the guyropes in the dew. He resented it. He resented Kialan, and he wished Dagner joy of him. It was hard to tell if Dagner got on with Kialan or not, because he was such an untalkative person. Dagner was like Lenina in that way. It was quite impossible to tell what Lenina thought about Kialan—or, indeed, about anything else.

Kialan, in spite of Clennen's rebuke, seemed unable to stop making outspoken remarks. "You know, that cart is really horribly garish," he said, on the second morning. Perhaps he had some excuse. It was standing against the dawn sky, as he saw it, and Moril's red head was just emerging from it. The effect was undeniably colourful, but Brid was keenly offended.

"It isn't!" she said.

"I expect you're too young to have much taste," Kialan replied. Brid swore to Moril that she was Kialan's enemy for life after that one.

What Moril resented most—apart from Kialan's elbows and the fact that Kialan never made the slightest attempt to help with any of the chores—was the superior way Kialan stood by and listened in whenever Moril had a music lesson. Unfortunately, he had them fairly frequently in the next few days. They were taking—perhaps for Kialan's benefit—a more direct route to Flennpass and the North than usual. It meant that they did not pass through any large towns and only two villages. Lenina bought supplies in the first, but they did not perform in either. Clennen took the opportunity to grind away at the old songs with Moril, to keep Brid hard at the panhorn, and to rehearse a number of songs with all of them.

Kialan stood by and put Moril off continually. Moril came so to resent it that he took refuge in more than usual vagueness. He would sit on his perch behind the driving-seat, staring up the white road unreeling ahead between the grey-green slopes of the South, basking in the hot sun—which never tanned him however long he sat in it—and dream of his birthplace in the North. It always saddened Moril that his father would never go to Hannart because of his disagreement with Earl Keril. He longed to see it, and he had built up in his mind a complete image of what it was like. There was an old grey castle in it, rowan trees, and blue hills of a certain spiky shape. Moril saw it clearly. He saw the whole North with it, spread over the grey-green Southern landscape as if it were painted on a window: dark woods and emerald dales, the queer green roads from olden days which led to places that were not important any longer, hard grey rocks, and the great waterfall at Drop-water. In it lived all the stories of magic and adventure that seemed to go with the North. The South had nothing to compare with them.

Hearing Kialan talking behind him, Moril thought that the North had one new advantage. Kialan would leave them there.

"I've said that six times now," Kialan said. "Do you spend *all* your time a thousand miles away?"

Moril was annoyed. His family could accuse him of dreaminess if they wanted, but Kialan was a stranger. "You've no right to say that," he said.

It was possible Kialan did not realise how annoyed Moril was. "You see," Brid explained to him later, a good long way behind the cart, "even when you're angry, you always look so sleepy and—and *milky*, that he probably didn't even notice you were attending. Not," she added tartly, "that he'd have noticed anybody's feelings but his own, mind you."

What Kialan had replied was: "Oh, good grief! I know you're the fool of the family by now, but you don't have to be rude as well as stupid!"

"And the same to you!" Moril retorted and took Kialan completely by surprise by butting him in the stomach. Kialan fell backwards heavily—and painfully, Moril hoped—onto the winejar. Where-upon Moril found the prudent thing to do was to hop out of the cart double quick and scud off down the road behind it. And for the rest of the day he was forced to walk well in the rear for fear of Kialan's vengeance.

But it was Clennen who took the vengeance. When they camped for the night, he beckoned both

Kialan and Moril up to him. "Are you two going to make up and apologise?" he enquired. Moril looked warily at Kialan and Kialan looked most unlovingly back. Neither answered. "Very well then," said Clennen, and banged their heads together. Nothing seems harder than another person's head. Moril could only hope that Kialan had seen as many stars as he had. He was rather surprised that Kialan did not say anything to Clennen. "Next time, I'll do it harder," Clennen promised. Then, as if nothing had happened, he went on to give Moril a lesson. And, to Moril's annoyance, Kialan stood by and listened just as usual.

The following day, they reached a market town called Crady and it came on to rain—big warm drops that seemed like part of the air and very little to do with the moist white sky. The raindrops made dark brown circles in the dust of the road and raised a delicious smell of wet earth. But it meant everyone crowding into the cart to change in great discomfort. Moril was not surprised that Kialan got out.

"I'm not really interested in your show," he said to Clennen. "I'll meet you on the other side of Crady, shall I?"

"If you like, lad," Clennen said cheerfully. Brid and Moril exchanged seething glances in the hot dim space under the cover and wondered why Clennen did not box Kialan's ears for him. But the only thing which seemed to perturb Clennen was the rain. "We shall have no audience in the open," he said. "I'll see what I can do. We'll go in with the cover up."

It was lucky that they did. By the time they came to the market place the rain was coming in white rods and bouncing up off the flagstones. Olob was wearing his most long-suffering expression and there was not a soul in sight. But Clennen had friends in Crady, just as he had everywhere else. Half an hour later, they were installed under the great beams of a warehouse on the corner of the market place, and a crowd, damp but interested, was gathering into it.

They gave an indoor kind of show. After Clennen had told everyone about Hadd and Henda, the Waywold money, the price on the Porter's head and the cost of corn in Derent, and the usual messages had been handed out, they sang songs with a chorus that the audience could join in. Dagner did his part early. Then, when good humour and attention were at their peak, Clennen told one of the old tales. This pleased Moril highly. He always felt rather too hot indoors, and playing the cwidder made him hotter still. But, during a tale, he was only needed once or twice. All the stories had places where there was a song. For the rest of the time Moril could sit on the dusty chaff of the floor with his arms wrapped round his knees and drink the story in.

Clennen chose to tell a branch of the story of the Adon. It had to be only a branch, because, as Clennen was fond of saying, stories clustered round the Adon and Osfameron like bees swarming. The songs which came in where the story needed them were the Adon's own, or Osfameron's. Moril always thought the old songs sounded rather better set in their proper stories, though he still wished the silly fellows had tried to sing more naturally. But their doings made splendid tales. Moril listened avidly to how Lagan wounded the Adon and the wound would not heal until Manaliabrid came out of the East to him. Then came the story of the love of both Lagan and the Adon for Manaliabrid, and how the Adon fled with her to the South. Lagan followed, but Osfameron helped them by singing a certain song in the passes of the mountains, so that the mountains walked and blocked the way through. And Lagan was forced to turn back.

Here Clennen lowered his rich voice to say: "I shall not sing you the song Osfameron sang then, for fear of moving the mountains again. But it is true that, since that day, the only pass to the North is Flennpass."

The Adon for a time roamed the South with Manaliabrid, singing for a living, until Lagan found where they were. Then he stole away Kastri, the Adon's son by his first wife, and the Adon followed. But Lagan was something of a magician. He made Kastri invisible and took on the shape of Kastri himself. And when the Adon came up to him, unsuspecting, Lagan stabbed him through the heart.

Here came Manaliabrid's lament, which Moril was supposed to sing. He took up his cwidder for it, glancing as he did so into the warm blue-grey depths of the barn at the attentive audience. To his surprise, Kialan was there. He was standing at the back, very wet and draggled, listening with as much interest as anyone there. Moril supposed he had decided he preferred a performance to a soaking after all. And he was annoyed with Kialan for coming. His head was full of grand things, journeys,

31

flights, fighting, and the magic North of once-upon-a-time. Kialan was the everyday world with a vengeance. Moril felt as if he had a foot on two different worlds, which were spinning apart from one another. It was not a pleasant feeling. He took his eyes off Kialan and concentrated on his cwidder.

Then Clennen went on to how Manaliabrid asked Osfameron for help. Osfameron sang, and made Kastri visible. Then he took up his cwidder and journeyed by a way that only he knew, to the borders of the Dark Land. There he played such music that all the dead crowded in multitudes to hear him. Once they were gathered, Osfameron sang and called the soul of the Adon to him. And—this part always gave Moril a delicious shiver—Clennen once more lowered his voice to say: "I shall not sing you the song Osfameron sang then, for fear of calling the dead again."

Osfameron led the Adon's soul back and restored it to his body. The Adon arose, defeated Lagan and reigned as the last king of Dalemark. He was the last king, because Manaliabrid's son, who was to have been king after him, chose instead to go back to his mother's country. "And since that time," said Clennen, "there have been no kings in Dalemark. Nor will there be, until the sons of Manaliabrid return."

Moril gave an entranced sigh. He had hardly the heart, after such a story, to join in *Jolly Holanders*, and he only managed to sing with an effort. After it, he crept away to the other end of the barn to avoid the usual crowd, and sat under the cart, brooding, while Clennen greeted his friends and Dagner failed to explain how he made up songs. If only such things happened nowadays! Moril thought. It seemed such a waste to be descended from the singer Osfameron, who knew the Adon and could call up the dead, and to live such a dull life. The world had gone so ordinary. Compare the Adon, who lived such a splendid life, with the present-day Earl of Hannart, who could think of nothing better to do than to stir up a rebellion, so that he dared not show his face in the South. Or you only had to think of the difference between that Osfameron, Moril brooded, and this one, Osfameron Tanamoril, to see how very plain and ordinary people had become lately. If only—

Here the plain and ordinary life interrupted in the person of Lenina, carrying the chinking hat to the cart. She was followed by the usual kind of murmuring gentleman. "And it must be sixteen years now—" this gentleman was murmuring.

"Seventeen," Lenina said briskly. "Moril, come out of that dream and count this money."

Moril unwillingly scrambled out from under the cart. As he did so, Clennen turned his head and his voice boomed across the barn. "No, I didn't care for him at all, last time I was in Neathdale." With his voice came a look that caused the murmuring gentleman to wither away into the crowd. Moril watched him wither, a little puzzled. He seemed to be the twin of the murmuring gentleman in Derent.

The takings were not bad, which pleased Lenina. And Clennen was in good humour because an old friend of his had made him a present of a beefsteak. It was beautifully red and tender and wrapped in leaves to keep it fresh. Clennen stowed it carefully in a locker. He talked jovially of supper as they drove through Crady in the slackening drizzle. Kialan, to Brid's contempt, was waiting for them under a tree just beyond the town.

"Huh!" said Brid. "Not interested in our shows, isn't Mr High-And-Mighty! Did you see him, Moril? Drinking in every word!"

"Yes," said Moril.

While the red steak fizzled over the fire, Brid said mock-innocently to Kialan: "Father told one of the Adon stories at the show. Do you know them at all?"

"Yes. And a dead bore they are too," said Kialan. "All that magic!"

"You would say that!" said Moril. "I saw—"

"Silence!" said Clennen. "You're interrupting the steak. Not another word until it's ready to eat."

The steak was certainly worthy of respect. Even Kialan had nothing to say against it. They went on again after supper. In his carefree way, Clennen seemed to be quite as anxious as Moril to see the North again. He refused to let Olob choose them a meadow until the sun was nearly down and the sky ahead and to the left was a mass of lilac clouds barred with red.

"Imagine *that* over the peaks of the North Dales," he said. "But even in the South, Mark Wood is fine at this time of year. There's nothing to beat a tall beech in spring. And do you know the Marsh at all, Kialan?"

"A little," said Kialan.

"If we'd time, I'd take you through it just for the flowers," said Clennen. "But it's too far east, more's the pity. The ducks there make your mouth water."

"There are rabbits in the South Dales," Dagner suggested.

"So there are," said Clennen. "Look the snares out tomorrow."

By the end of the following day, the landscape had begun to change. The rolling grey-green slopes gave way to higher, greener hills, and there were more trees. It was like a foretaste of the North. Moril began to feel pleasantly excited, although he knew that they were only entering the South Dales. Tholian, Earl of the South Dales, was reputed to be a tyrant fiercer even than Henda. It was still a long way to the North. Beyond these green hills lay the Uplands and Mark Wood, before they came to Flennpass and the North at last.

Nevertheless, budding apple trees made a pleasant change from rows of vines. The nights were slightly cooler and rabbits were plentiful. Every night Dagner went off to set snares round about the camp and, to Moril's surprise, Kialan made his first helpful gesture and went with Dagner.

"It's only because he likes killing things," Brid said. "He's that type."

Whatever the reason, Kialan was surprisingly good at catching and skinning rabbits, and Lenina was good at rabbit stew. Since they had wine as well, they fed very well for the next few days. Moril was almost grateful to Kialan. But Brid was not in the least grateful, because every time they stopped in a town or village to give a show, Kialan would put on his act of not being interested and announce that he would meet them outside the town. And every time, unfailingly, they would see him among the audience, as interested as anyone there.

"Two-faced hypocrite!" Brid said indignantly. "He's just trying to make us feel small."

"That wouldn't do you any harm," Lenina said, in her dry way. Brid was more indignant than ever. It was becoming clear that Lenina rather approved of Kialan. Not that she said anything. It was more that she did not say any of the things she might have done. And when Kialan tore his good coat in the wood, Lenina mended it for him with careful neat stitches.

Kialan seemed far more surprised than grateful when Lenina handed him the mended coat. "Oh— thanks," he said. "You shouldn't have bothered." His face was red, and he seemed actually a little scornful of Lenina for doing it.

"Nothing to what I am!" said Brid. "He can go in rags for all I care."

The day after this, they entered the part of the South Dales which was the lordship of Markind. They never gave shows in Markind. Brid's dislike of Kialan came to a head while Olob was patiently dragging the cart up and down the steep little hills of this lordship. The reason was that Clennen, who never disdained an audience, began to explain to Kialan exactly why he always hurried through Markind without giving a performance.

"I took Lenina from here, you see," he said. "From the very middle of Markind, out of the Lord's own hall. Didn't I, Lenina?"

"You did," said Lenina. She always looked very non-committal whenever Clennen told this story.

"She was betrothed to the Lord's son. What was his name? Pennan—that was it. And a wet young idiot he was too," Clennen said reminiscently.

"I was asked in to sing at the betrothal—I had quite a name, even in those days, and I was a good deal in demand for occasions like that, let me tell you. Well, no sooner did I come into the hall and set eyes on Lenina, than I knew she was the woman for me. Wasted on that idiot Fenner. That was his name, wasn't it, Lenina?"

"He was called Ganner," said Lenina.

"Oh, yes," said Clennen. "I remember he reminded me of a goose somehow. It must have been the name. I'd thought it was his scraggy neck, or those button eyes of his. Anyway, I thought I'd rely on my looks being better than his and deal with Master Gosler later. For the first thing, I concentrated on Lenina. I sang—I've never sung better, before or since—and Lenina here couldn't take her eyes off me. Well, I don't blame her, because I don't mind admitting that I was a fine-looking man in those days, and gifted too—which Flapper wasn't. So I asked Lenina in a song whether she'd marry me instead of this Honker fellow, and when I came up to get my reward for my singing, she said Yes. So then I dealt with him. I turned to him. 'Lording,' I said, most respectful, 'Lording, what gift will you give me?' And he said 'Anything you want. You're a great singer'— which was the only sensible thing he said that evening. So I said, 'I'll take what you have in your right hand.' He was holding Lenina's hand, you see. I still laugh when I think of the look on his face."

While the story went on—and it made a long one, for Clennen went over it several times, embroidering the details—Brid and Moril walked by the roadside out of earshot, watching the fed-up look settle on Kialan's face. They had both heard the story more times than they could remember.

"I suppose the thing about being a singer is that you like telling the same story a hundred times," Brid said rather acidly. "But you'd think Father would remember Ganner's name by this time."

"That's all part of it," said Moril. "I always wonder," he added dreamily, "what would happen if we met Ganner, while we were going through Markind. Would he arrest Father?"

"Of course he wouldn't," said Brid. "I don't suppose it's true anyway. And even if it did happen, Ganner must have grown into a big fat lord by now and forgotten Mother ever existed."

Since this was Brid's true opinion of the matter, it was a little unreasonable of her to be so angry when she found Kialan shared it. But one is seldom reasonable when one dislikes someone. They stopped for lunch, and Clennen, thoroughly in his stride, went on embroidering the story.

"Lenina's a real lady," he said, leaning comfortably against the pink and scarlet wheel of the cart. "She's Tholian's niece, you know. But he cast her off for running away with me. And it was all my fault for playing that trick on Gander. 'Lording,' I said to him, 'give me what you have in your right hand.' Oh, I shall never forget his face! Never!" And he burst out laughing.

Kialan had heard this at least three times by then. Moril had rarely seen him look so fed up. While Clennen was laughing, Kialan got up quickly to avoid hearing any more, and stumped off without looking where he was going. He nearly fell over

Moril and Brid and became more fed up than ever.

"Blinking bore your father is!" he said. "I'd be quite sorry for Ganner if I thought there was a word of truth in it!"

"How dare you!" said Brid. "How *dare* you say that! I've a good mind to punch your nose in!"

"I don't fight with girls," Kialan said loftily. "All I meant was I'm sick of hearing about Ganner. If your father remembers it that well, why on earth can't he get the poor fellow's name right?"

"It's part of the *story!*" screamed Brid, and threw herself at Kialan.

Kialan, for a second or so, tried to keep up his claim not to fight girls, with the result that Brid punched his nose twice and then boxed his ears in perfect freedom. "You spiteful cat!" said Kialan and grabbed both her wrists. It was in self-defence. On the other hand, he squeezed her wrists so painfully that he hurt Brid rather more than if he had hit her. She lashed out at his legs with her bare feet, but, finding that made no impression on Kialan, she sank her teeth into the hand round her wrists. At this, Kialan lost his temper completely and punched Brid with his free hand.

Dagner never let people hit Brid. He surged up from his seat in the hedgerow and fell on Kialan. Moril, since Dagner seemed to be doing his best to strangle Kialan, thought he had better get Brid out from between them and entered the fray too. They made a grunting furious bundle. Brid would not unfasten her teeth and Kialan would not let go of Brid. Clennen heaved himself up, strolled over and wrenched Dagner away from Kialan and Kialan away from Brid. Everyone, including

Moril, fell with heavy thumps, this way and that. Clennen might have been fat, but he was also strong.

"Now stop!" said Clennen. "And if you've anything more to say about my story, Kialan, say it to me." He looked cheerfully down at Kialan angrily sprawled on the roadside sucking his bleeding knuckles. "Well?"

"All right!" said Kialan. "All *right*!" Moril could see he was nearly crying. Brid was crying. "You can keep on saying you'll never forget Ganner—or whatever he's called—all you like," said Kialan. "I don't believe you've even met him! You wouldn't know him if he came walking down the road this minute! So there!"

The cheerfulness died out of Clennen's face. It was replaced by a very odd look. Kialan noticeably tensed at it. "Do you know Ganner, then?" Clennen said.

"No, of course I don't!" said Kialan. "How could I? I don't suppose he exists."

"Oh, he exists all right," said Clennen. "And I'm sure you don't know him. Yet you're right. I've seen Ganner three times this month and not known him till this minute." He laughed again, and Kialan relaxed considerably. "Not a face that stands out in a crowd," he said. "Eh, Lenina?"

"I suppose not," agreed Lenina, and continued calmly slicing cold sausage.

"*You* knew him though, didn't you?" Clennen said. "In Derent, and on the road, and again in Crady?"

"Not till he said who he was," Lenina said, quite unperturbed.

There seemed suddenly to be a situation ten times worse. All through lunch, Clennen looked at Lenina in a tense, troubled way. He seemed to be expecting her to say something and, at the same time, carefully not saying all sorts of things himself. And Lenina said nothing. She said nothing so positively and obviously that the air seemed sticky with her silence. It was hateful. The rest of them picked awkwardly at their food, and no one spoke much. Kialan did not say anything. It was obvious, even to Brid, that he was kicking himself for causing the situation—as well he might, Moril thought.

When the food was finished and the cart packed again, they went on, still in the same heavy silence. At last, Clennen could bear it no longer.

"Lenina," he said, "you're not regretting all that, are you? If you want that kind of life—if you'd rather have Ganner—just say the word and I'll turn Olob towards Markind this moment."

Moril gasped. Brid's mouth came open in her tearstained face. They looked at Clennen and found he seemed quite serious. Then they looked at Lenina, expecting her to laugh. It was so silly. Lenina was as much part of their life as Olob or the cart. But Lenina did not laugh, nor did she say anything. Not only Brid and Moril, but Dagner, Kialan and Clennen too, stared at her in increasing anxiety.

They came to a fork in the road. One branch led west, and the milestone said *Markind 10*. "Do I turn here?" asked Clennen.

Lenina gave herself an impatient shake. "Oh no," she said. "Clennen Mendakersson, you must be a very big fool indeed to think such a thing of me."

Clennen burst into a roll of relieved laughter. He shook the reins and Olob trotted past the turning. "I must say," he said, laughing still, "I can't see how you could prefer Ganner to me. He couldn't have made the songs I've made to you, not if his life depended on it."

"Then why did you think I did?" Lenina asked coldly. The trouble was not over yet.

"Well," Clennen said awkwardly. "Money and all that. And it's what you were bred to, after all."

"I see," said Lenina. There was silence again for quite half an hour, except for the plopping of Olob's hooves and the light rumble of the cart. Kialan was unable to bear it. He got out and walked ahead, whistling the *Second March* rather defiantly. The others sat with their heads hanging, wishing Lenina would make peace. At last she said, "Oh, Clennen, do stop sitting there watching me like a dog! I'm not going to take wings and fly, am I? It's lucky Olob has more sense than you, or we'd be in the ditch by now!"

Then the trouble seemed to be over. Clennen was shortly laughing and talking again. And Lenina, if she was silent, was silent in her usual way, which everyone was used to. Brid and Moril got out of the cart too, though they did not go near Kialan. Brid was still too angry with him.

Chapter IV

That night they camped in one of the many little valleys Markind abounded in. There were woods up its steep sides and a meadow in the bottom, containing a small peaceful lake full of newly-hatched tadpoles. Dagner and Kialan went off to set their snares. Lenina put herbs on the fire against the midges, and the fragrant smoke streamed sideways and settled across the lake in bands. Brid and Moril, quite unworried by insects, waded into the shallows of the lake and tried enthusiastically to collect tadpoles in an old picklejar. Moril had just lost most of them by accident, when he looked up to find his father watching them.

"You want a bigger jar," Clennen said. "And both of you want to remember what I said to Kialan about give and take."

"*He* doesn't remember it," Brid said sulkily.

"He's never had to learn it before," said Clennen. "That's his trouble. But it's not yours, Brid. A fight takes two."

"Did you hear what he said?" Moril demanded.

"I'm not deaf," said Clennen. "He's entitled to his opinion, like everyone else. And it wouldn't hurt you to find some opinions of your own instead of borrowing Brid's, Moril. Now get that slime off your fingers before you touch my cwidder."

While Moril was having his lesson, Kialan came out of the woods and into the lake, where he tried to teach Dagner to swim. The sight of them splashing about was a great distraction to Moril. It grew worse when Kialan tried to persuade Brid to learn to swim too. Brid claimed to be afraid of leeches. Nothing would induce her to go above her knees in water, but she agreed to learn the arm-movements. Moril could hear her laughing. It looked as if Kialan was trying to make friends.

Moril became more distracted than ever. Perhaps, after all, Kialan was not bad at heart—only tactless. Moril tried to decide what he thought. It really rankled with him that Clennen believed he borrowed Brid's opinions. Moril considered that he thought long and deeply—if rather vaguely—about most things. But he knew he had agreed with Brid, quite unquestioningly, both about Kialan and about the Ganner story. And it looked as if Brid had been wrong about both. Moril did not know what he thought.

"I suppose I ought to be used to you being up in the clouds by now," said Clennen. "Do you want to swim too?"

"No," said Moril. "Yes. I mean, is that story about Ganner true, then?"

"Word of honour," said Clennen. "Except it's the fellow's face I seem to have forgotten, not his name. I may embroider a detail here and there, but I never tell a story that isn't true, Moril. Remember that. Now go and swim if you want to."

Clennen was clearly very relieved that Lenina was not leaving for Markind. He drank a great deal of the wine that night to celebrate. The level in the huge bottle was almost down to the straw basket when he finally rolled into the larger tent and fell asleep. He was still asleep next morning when Dagner and Kialan went off to look at their snares. When Brid and Moril got up, they could hear him snoring, though Lenina was up and combing out her soft fair hair by the lake. Brid attended to the fire, and Moril tried to attend to Olob. Olob, for some reason, was tetchy. He kept flinging up his head and shying at shadows.

"What's the matter with him?" Moril asked his mother.

Lenina's comb had hit a tangle. She was lugging at it fiercely and not really attending. "No idea," she said. "Leave him be."

So Moril left off trying to groom Olob and turned to put the currycomb back in the cart. He found himself looking at a number of men, who were pushing their way through the last of the wood into the clear space by the lake. They were out almost as soon as Moril saw them, six of them. They stood in a group, looking at Moril, Brid kneeling by the fire, Lenina by the lake, the cart and the tents.

"Clennen the singer," one of them said. "Where is he?"

Olob tossed his head and trotted away round the lake.

"He's not here," said Brid.

Moril thought he would have said the same. The men alarmed him. It was odd to see six well-dressed men outside a wood in the middle of nowhere. They were very well-dressed. They wore cloth as good as Kialan's coat, and all of them had that sleek look that comes from always living in style.

Each of them wore a sword in a well-kept leather scabbard, belted over the good cloth of their coats, and Moril did not like the way the hilts of those swords looked smooth with frequent use. But the truly alarming thing about them was that they had an air of purpose, all of them, which hit Moril like a gust of cold wind and frightened him.

"My father won't be back for ages," he said, hoping they would go away.

"Then we'll wait for him," said the man who had asked. Moril liked him least of all. He was fair and light-eyed, and there was an odd look in those eyes which Moril did not trust.

Lenina evidently felt the same. "Suppose you give me your message for Clennen," she said, coming forward with her hair still loose.

"You wouldn't like it, lady," said the man. "We'll wait."

"Moril," said Lenina. "Go round the lake and fetch your father."

Moril thought that was clever of her. It would deceive the men, and Dagner and Kialan might be some help. He tossed the currycomb into the cart and set off at a trot. But Clennen chose that moment to crawl out of the tent like a badger. He stood up, with his eyes red and blinking inside a tousled frill of hair and beard.

"Somebody call me?" he said sleepily.

Moril stopped, helpless. Everything went so quickly that he could hardly believe it was happening. The six men pushed forward in a body, overwhelming Lenina for a moment, and then leaving her in the open, clutching Brid. Their swords caught the pink early sun. The group round

46

Clennen trampled a bit. Clennen, sleepy as he was, must have put up something of a fight. A man stumbled sideways into the lake. Another fell in with a splash. Then the six men, swords sheathed again, went running away from the lake in a group. One glanced into Clennen's tent and then the smaller one. Another took a quick look into the cart as they passed.

"Nothing here," he called.

"Look in the woods then," said the fair one. And they were gone.

Clennen lay where he had fallen, half in the lake with blood running out of him into the water.

Before Moril could move, there was a thumping of racing feet. Dagner shot past him round the lake and surged on to his knees in the water beside Clennen. "Have they killed him?"

"Not quite," said Lenina. "Help me move him."

Moril stood where he was, some distance away, and watched them heave his father out of the calm sunny water. Brid's face was greyish white and her teeth were chattering. Dagner's mouth kept twisting about. Moril could see his hands shaking. But Lenina was quite calm and no paler than usual. As they turned Clennen over, Moril saw a cut in his chest. Bright red blood was gushing from it as fast as the river ran in Dropwater, steaming a little in the cold air over the surface of the lake.

At the sight, the bright trees, the lake and the sunny sky dipped and swung in front of Moril. Everything turned sour and grey and distant. He could not move from the spot. Up in the woods behind him, he could dimly hear the six men crashing about and calling to one another, but they could have been on the moon for all the fear and interest Moril felt. His eyes stared, so widely that they hurt, at the group by the water.

Lenina, without abating her calm, tore a big strip from her petticoat, and another, to stop the bleeding. "Give me yours," she said to Brid and, while Brid, shaking and shivering, was getting out of her petticoat, Lenina said in the same calm way to Dagner, "Get the small flask from the cart."

Moril stared at his mother working and telling Brid what to do. The only sign of emotion Lenina showed was when her hair trailed in the way of the bandages. "Bother the stuff!" she said. "Brid, tie it back for me."

Brid was still trying to get a ribbon round Lenina's hair when Dagner scudded back with the flask. "Do you think you can save him?" he asked, as if he were pleading with Lenina.

She looked up at him calmly. "No, Dagner. The most I can do is keep him with you for a while. He'll want to have his say. He always did." She took the flask from Dagner and uncorked it.

Moril desolately watched her trying to get some of the liquid from the flask into Clennen's mouth. It was not fair. He felt it was not fair of his father at all, to die like this, first thing in the morning, miles from anywhere. He ought to have had warning. Dying was a thing someone like Clennen ought to do properly, in front of a crowd, with music playing if possible.

Music was possible, of course. Moril found himself beside the cart, without quite knowing how he had got there. He scrambled up and seized the nearest cwidder. It happened to be the big one.

In the ordinary way, Moril would not have chosen it. But being inside the cart made him feel sick and queer, so he simply took what came first to hand and backed hastily down with it.

While he was getting its strap over his back, he realised that Clennen's eyes were open. And it was clear that Clennen shared Moril's opinion. Moril heard him say, rather thickly, but quite strongly: "This came out of the blue, didn't it? I'd have preferred to have notice."

Moril put his hands to the strings and began to play, very softly, the weird broken little tune of *Manaliabrid's Lament*. The cwidder responded sweetly. The old song seemed more melodious than usual and, because of the water, it carried out across the lake until the valley seemed full of it. Moril heard its echo from the woods opposite.

His ears were so full of the sound that he did not hear much else of what Clennen said. Clennen's voice became weaker, anyway, after that first remark, and he spoke to Lenina in what was only a murmur. Then he spoke to Brid for a while, reaching out to hold her hand, which made Brid cry. After that, it was Dagner's turn. Clennen was very weak by then. Dagner had to put his head right down near his father's face in order to hear him. Moril played on, as softly as he could, watching Dagner listening and nodding, and wondered vaguely at the amount Clennen seemed to have to say. Then Dagner looked up and beckoned to Moril.

"He wants to talk to you. Quickly."

Moril did not dare take off the cwidder for fear of wasting time. He hurried over to Clennen with it bumping at his thighs and knees, and hoisted it away sideways as he knelt down. Clennen's face was paler than Moril had ever seen a face before. His eyes did not seem to reflect the sky, or Moril bending over him, though it was clear he could see Moril.

"Got the big cwidder, have you?" Clennen said. Moril nodded. He could not manage to speak. "Keep it carefully," said Clennen. "It's yours now. Always meant to give it to you, Moril, because I think you've got the ability. Or will have. But you have to come to terms with it, and with yourself. Understand?" Moril nodded again, though he did not understand in the least. "You're in two halves at present," Clennen went on. "Often thought so. Come together, Moril, and there's no knowing what you might do. There's power in that cwidder, if you can use it. Used to be Osfameron's. He could use it. Handed down to me. I couldn't use it. Only found the power once, when I—" Clennen paused for breath. Moril waited for him to go on, but nothing happened. Clennen stayed as he was, with his eyes open looking at Moril, and his lips parted. After a while, Moril realised that this was all there would be. He got up and carefully, very carefully, put the cwidder back in its place inside the cart.

Brid was crying loudly. Lenina was standing very upright beside the lake, as calm as ever. Dagner seemed to have frozen into the same sort of calmness, facing her. And Kialan was coming slowly towards them round the lake with a bundle of dead rabbits.

When he reached them, Kialan stopped. He looked at Clennen and, for once, seemed not to know what to say. "I'm—terribly sorry," he said at length.

"It was going to happen some time," said Lenina. "Will you help us dig a grave, please."

"Of course," said Kialan. "Here?"

"Why not?" said Lenina. "Clennen never had a home after he left Hannart, and we can't take him there."

"Very well," said Kialan, and he laid the rabbits down and unhooked the spade from its clips beneath the cart. Dagner went and fetched the pick-axe, and the two set to work. Lenina watched and seemed ready to take Kialan's advice, as if, in some odd way, Kialan was in charge just then. "I think we should mark the spot," Kialan said as he dug.

"How?" said Lenina.

"Is there a spare board in the cart?" Kialan asked.

"Find him one, Moril," said Lenina.

Moril managed to work free one of the spare boards Clennen always carried under the floor of the cart and, on Kialan's instructions, he sawed off a piece about three feet long. Then he relieved Kialan at the digging for a while. Kialan took out his sheath-knife and carved away at the board, quickly and competently, as if this was another thing he was good at. When he had finished, the board had letters deeply and neatly cut into it. *CLENNEN THE SINGER.*

"That do?" said Kialan.

"Very well," said Lenina.

When the grave was ready, Kialan, Dagner and Brid put Clennen into it. Moril did not like to see his father topple into the hole. Nor did he like to see the earth going in on top of Clennen's face and clothes. Rather than watch, he fetched his own cwidder and stood back a little, playing another lament, a newer one that had been made for an earl of Dropwater killed in battle. He went on playing while Brid put the turf back in place and Kialan trenched his board in until it was standing upright at the head of the grave, as it should. And now that there was nothing but a grave to be seen, Moril began to feel that something was missing. They should all be feeling and doing something else. They should be angry. Clennen had been murdered. They should be trying to bring the murderers to justice. But none of them thought of it. It was out of the question, here in the South. The six men had been far too well-dressed.

"There," said Kialan, wiping his hands on his coat.

"Thank you," said Lenina. "Now I must change. This dress has blood on it. And you too, Brid. Kialan, I think it would be a good idea if you changed your coat for Dagner's old one."

Kialan agreed to this, although Moril did not think Kialan's good coat was more than a little earthy. When everyone was changed and cleaned, Lenina told Dagner to catch Olob and harness him to the cart. Kialan picked up his bundle of rabbits.

"Leave those," said Lenina. "We don't need them."

"Well, I don't fancy them at the moment, either," said Kialan. "But—"

"Leave them," said Lenina. Kialan did as he was bid. Now Lenina seemed to be definitely in charge. It was she who took the reins when Olob was ready and drove out of the valley.

Brid and Moril looked back. It was a very beautiful valley. Probably, Moril thought, it was a good place to be buried, if one had to be. Brid cried. Dagner did not look back. He had sunk into a silence as profound as any of Lenina's. He did not look at anything, and no one liked to speak to him.

Lenina drove northwards for a mile or so, until she came to a road that turned off to the left. Then, to Moril's surprise, she swung the cart into it.

"Hey! Where are we going?" said Moril.

"Markind," said Lenina.

"What? Not to Ganner!" demanded Brid, halting in the middle of a sob.

"Yes. To Ganner," said Lenina. "He said he would have me and mine if ever I was free, and I know he meant it."

"Oh but, no! You can't!" said Moril. "Not just like that!"

"Why not?" Lenina asked. "How do you think we shall live, without a singer to earn us money?"

"We can manage," said Moril. "I can sing. Dagner can—Dagner—" His voice tailed away as he thought of Dagner and himself trying to perform as Clennen did. He just could not see Dagner doing it. He did not know what to say, so he stopped, fearing he might be hurting Dagner's feelings. But it looked as if Dagner was not listening. "Father wouldn't like us to go to Markind," Moril asserted. He was sure of that, at least.

"I can't see that your father has much say in the matter now," Lenina answered drily. "Get this clear, Moril. I know well enough that your father was a good man, and the best singer in Dalemark, and I've done my duty by him for seventeen years.

53

That's half my lifetime, Moril. I've gone barefoot and learned to cook and make music. I've lived in a cart in all weathers, and never complained. I've mended and cleaned and looked after you all. There were things your father did that I didn't agree with at all, but I never argued with him or crossed him. I did my duty exactly in every way, and I've nothing to reproach myself with. But Clennen's dead now, so I'm free to do as I choose. What I'm choosing is my birthright and yours too. Do you understand?"

"I suppose so," Moril mumbled. He had never heard Lenina say anything like this before. He was frightened and rather shocked to see that she must have been *not* saying it for longer than he had lived. He thought it was wrong of her, but he could not have said why. He thought she was altogether wrong, but he could not find any words to set against her. All he could do was to exchange a scared, helpless look with Brid. Brid said nothing either.

It was Kialan who spoke. He sounded rather embarrassed. "It's not my place to object," he said. "But I do have to get to Hannart, Lenina."

"I know," said Lenina. "I've thought of that. You can pose as my son for the moment, and I'll find someone to take you North as soon as I can, I promise. Hestefan's in the South, I know, and Fredlan may be too."

Kialan looked exasperated as well as embarrassed. "But Ganner must know how many children you've got!"

"I shouldn't think so," Lenina said calmly. "People who haven't got children themselves never bother to count other people's. If he wonders, I'll say you've been ill and we'd left you at Fledden."

Kialan sighed. "Oh well. Thanks anyway."

"Remember that," Lenina said to Moril, Brid and Dagner, and Moril felt very queer, because "Remember that" was such a favourite saying of Clennen's. "Kialan's your brother. If anyone asks, he's been ill in Fledden."

Olob plodded towards Markind. He did not look happy either, Moril thought, looking at the droop of Olob's head. Moril was so miserable himself that he could almost hear it, like a droning in his ears, and he could not hide away in vagueness, much as he tried. He felt vividly and horribly attentive to everything, from the leaves in the hedge to the shape of Kialan's nose. Kialan's eagle-nose was so different from Dagner's, Brid's or Moril's that surely anyone could tell at a glance he was no relation? Why did he have to be a relation anyway? And had Clennen known he wanted to go to Hannart? Clennen would not have gone there, because he never went to Hannart. And why had the six men killed Clennen? Who were they, and what were they looking for in the wood? And why, why, why above all, had Clennen given Moril a cwidder he did not want in the least?

I shall never play it, Moril thought. I'll polish it and string it, and maybe tune it from time to time, but I don't want to play it. I know I should be grateful, because it must be very valuable—though it *can't* be old enough to have belonged to Osfameron: he's long ago in a story—but I don't like it and I don't want it.

Markind came into view at the other end of a valley. Without meaning to, Moril looked at it as he always looked at a new town. Sleepy and respectable, he thought. Bad takings. Then he remembered he was supposed to be going here to live, not to sing, and tried very hard to look at the pile of yellowish-grey houses with interest. He found he was more interested in the villainously freckled cows which were grazing in the small green meadows outside the town.

Lenina looked at these cows with pleasure. "I remember I always liked those speckles," she said. She encouraged Olob to trot, and the grey and yellow houses approached swiftly. Moril's heart sank rather—and he had thought it was low enough before.

Soon they were winding up a gravelly street between quiet old houses. The houses were tall and cold and shuttered. There were very few people about. Even when they came to the main square and found a market going on under the high plane trees, there were still very few people, and these all sober citizens who looked at the gay cart with strong disapproval. Lenina drove past the stalls looking neither to right nor to left, and drew Olob up in front of a round-topped gateway in a massive yellow wall. Two men who seemed to be on guard at the gate peered round it at the cart in evident astonishment.

"Had you business here?" one of them asked Lenina.

"Certainly," Lenina answered haughtily. "Go and tell Ganner Sagersson that Lenina Thornsdaughter is here."

They looked at her in even more astonishment at that. But one of them went off into the spaces behind the thick yellow wall. The other stayed, frowning wonderingly at Lenina, the cart and her family, until Moril scarcely knew where to look.

"What's the betting we get a message back to say Not Today Thank You?" whispered Brid.

"Be quiet, Brid!" said Lenina. "Behave properly, can't you!"

Brid would have lost her bet. The man who had gone with the message came back at a run, and they could hear a number of people behind the gate, running too. The two halves of the gate were flung wide open.

"Please drive in," said the man.

Lenina smiled graciously and shook the reins. Olob plodded forward, disapproval in every line of his ears and back, into a small deep courtyard lined with interested faces. Ganner was standing in the middle of it, smiling delightedly.

"Welcome back, Lenina!" he said. "I never thought I'd see you so soon. What happened?"

"Some men killed Clennen this morning," said Lenina. "They looked like the pick of somebody's hearthmen to me."

"Not really!" exclaimed Ganner. Then he looked a little worried and asked, "Does that mean it happened in my lordship then?"

"Yes," said Lenina. "At Medmere."

"I'd better send some hearthmen over to investigate," said Ganner. "Anyway, come down and come in. Are these your children?"

"My three sons and my daughter," said Lenina.

"What a lot of them!" said Ganner, looking a little daunted. But he smiled gallantly at all four. "I'll do my best to look after you all," he said. Moril could not find it in his heart to dislike Ganner, much as he had intended to. It was so plain he meant well. If, to someone who had been used to Clennen, he seemed a very ordinary person, then that was hardly Ganner's fault, Moril supposed.

"He doesn't look much like a goose," Brid whispered, in some disappointment. Kialan had to bite his lip. Moril looked at Ganner gallantly helping Lenina down from the cart and smiling at her in a way that showed he adored her. Apart from that smile, he really seemed perfectly normal and ungooselike.

"Oh dear, oh dear!" Ganner exclaimed, as they all got down. "Shoes! Boots! Can you only afford one pair of boots?"

Lenina glanced along their line of bare feet, interrupted by Kialan's scuffed boots. "We don't usually bother with them," she explained. "But Collen has tender feet."

"I must make sure you all have shoes this instant!" Ganner exclaimed distractedly.

"You know, I think he may be a goose after all," Brid said, with considerable satisfaction.

Chapter V

By that afternoon, Moril was wondering if it was only that morning they had left Clennen buried by the lake. It felt like last century. There had been so many changes. After a good breakfast, followed by the attentions of a tailor, a bootmaker and Ganner's old nurse, followed in turn by an astonishingly good lunch, Moril scarcely knew himself. He looked in a mirror—it was a thing he seldom had the chance of doing, so he looked long and often—and he saw a smoothly-combed red-haired boy in a suit of good blue cloth and a pair of soft, rust-coloured boots. The boots, to tell the truth, pleased him enormously. But he did not look in the least like his idea of himself. Dagner and Kialan had become spruce, gentlemanly figures in the same kind of blue clothes, and Brid a young lady in bright cherry colour. They were all four behaving very soberly and politely, not because Ganner insisted on it— because he did not—but simply because Markind was the sort of place where you could behave in no other way.

The biggest change was to Lenina. She was splendidly dressed too, and she had done her hair the way ladies did. Her cheeks were pinker than usual, and she laughed and chattered and hurried about with Ganner on a hundred errands. Moril had not often seen her laugh, and he had certainly never seen her so talkative. She was like a different person. That troubled him. It troubled him far more than learning she was going to marry Ganner that same evening.

Moril quite liked Ganner. Ganner told Moril he could do just what he liked and go anywhere he wanted, and obviously meant it. He was a very good-natured man. Moril quite liked the other people in the house too. He liked Ganner's old nurse specially. She fussed rather, and she said rather too often that she had always known Lenina Thornsdaughter would come back to them, but she called Moril "my duck" and said he was a "blessing". And while she was dressing him, she told Moril a story about a lord of Markind who had been outlawed. Moril had not heard the story before, and he drank it up. But he felt strange. Everything felt strange.

Moril took Ganner at his word and explored the house. He found two gardens and the kitchens. He looked at the cellars and the small rooms under the roof, but in between each exploration he found himself drifting into the stable-yard. The cart had been put away in a coach-house there, just as it was, winejar, cwidders and all, down to the string of onions under the driving-seat. It was just the same, yet, somehow, it already looked smaller and dustier and a little faded. Moril spent a lot of time talking to Olob, who was standing dejectedly in a stall nearby and seemed glad of his company. Moril stole sugar for him from the kitchen, which was easy to do, because everyone there was in a great bustle, preparing for the wedding feast. Olob ate it politely, but he looked sad and he was sweating rather.

"Poor fellow," Moril said sadly. "I'm hot too. It's being in a house."

As the afternoon drew on, Moril became hotter still. Being between walls so oppressed him that he wondered whether to go out and walk in the town. But Markind had not inspired him with any wish to see more of it. He wandered to the stable-yard and then into one of the gardens. Brid was there. She was feeling much the same, for she had taken off her cherry-coloured boots and was sitting with her feet in one of the goldfish ponds.

They exchanged sad, polite smiles, and Moril went on into the second garden. Behind him, he heard Ganner's voice.

"My dear little girl! You'll catch your death like that! Do please dry your feet and put your boots on. You'll worry your mother."

Moril felt sorry for Brid. Then he suddenly felt even more—desperately—sorry for himself. He needed to be somewhere else, out in the open. He looked round wildly, upwards, everywhere. And a sturdy creeper growing up the thick yellow wall of the house gave him an idea. He slung himself on to it and started to climb.

It was extremely easy, except for the last bit, which needed a long stride and a heave across some crumbly stonework. Then he was on the wide, leaded roofs. It was splendid. Moril looked round, into the town, out across the valley, and over to valleys beyond. He turned north and looked at the misty blue peaks there, where he had so longed to go, and Kialan—lucky Kialan!—was going soon.

But that made him sad. So, presently, Moril began to patter about across the leads and among the chimneys. He skirted courtyards and looked down into the gardens. Then he ran along a narrow part to another wing and looked down into another court.

And there was Ganner, horrified and gesturing below. "Come down! Come down at once!"

Moril looked. There was a lead pipe and an easy flight of windows. Obediently, he swung his legs over the edge of the roof.

Ganner stopped him with a hoarse shriek. "No! Stop! Do you want to break your neck? Wait!" He ran away and presently ran back with a crowd of men carrying a ladder. With them ran a group of horrified maids, and the old nurse, wringing her hands.

"My duck! Oh, my duck!"

Moril sat sadly on the edge of the roof, swinging his legs and watching them all pothering with the ladder. He knew what was wrong with Ganner now. He was a fusspot.

The ladder finally thumped against the wall beside him. "You can come down now," Ganner called. "Go very carefully."

Moril sighed and got onto the ladder. He came down rather slowly out of sheer perverseness. He decided when he got near enough he would say to Ganner, "But you told me I could go anywhere I wanted." When he judged he was low enough for it to be most effective, he turned round to say it.

A man was just coming in through the door to the courtyard—a fair man with light, untrust-worthy eyes, who checked for a moment when he saw Moril twenty feet up a long ladder, staring at him. Shrugging slightly, the man strolled over to Ganner and said something to him. Ganner replied. The man shrugged again, said another word or so to Ganner, and strolled out of the courtyard.

Moril forgot what he intended to say. Instead, as soon as he was down on the ground, he said, "Who was that man here just now? The fair one, who spoke to you."

Ganner looked uneasy, so uneasy that Moril's chest went tight and he felt sick. "Oh—er—just someone who's my guest here," said Ganner. "Now you are absolutely *not* to get on the roof again! It's extremely high, and the leads are quite unsafe. You might have been killed!"

"Killed, my duck!" said his nurse.

Moril bore with a long scold from both Ganner and the nurse, without listening to a word. Both of them would have scolded anyway, but Moril was fairly sure that Ganner was scolding mostly as an excuse not to discuss the fair man. Moril did not want to discuss him. His one desire was to get away and find Lenina.

Lenina was in the great hall of the house. Presumably, it was the same place where Clennen had sung and then played the trick on Ganner seventeen years before. Lenina was gaily organizing the tables for the wedding-feast, and doing it as if she had done nothing else all her life. Moril had to pull her sleeve to get her to attend to him.

"Mother! One of the men who killed Father! He's staying here."

"Oh, Moril, don't interrupt me with stupid stories!" Lenina said impatiently.

"But I saw him," said Moril.

"You must have made a mistake," said Lenina. She pulled her sleeve away and went back to the tables.

Moril stood, shocked and troubled, in the middle of the hall. He saw quite clearly that his mother did not want to believe him. She had put Clennen and all that part of her life behind her and she did not want to be reminded of it. Yet, if Ganner had had a hand in killing Clennen, this was the last place she ought to be—the last place any of them ought to be. Moril looked at gay, busy Lenina, shook his head desolately, and hurried away to find Brid.

Brid was hurrying through the garden in the opposite direction. "Moril—!"

"One of the men who killed Father," said Moril. "He's staying here."

"I know. I saw him," said Brid. "Did you try to tell Mother?"

"Yes. She wouldn't listen."

"She wouldn't listen to me either," said Brid. "She doesn't want to know, I think. Moril, what are we going to do? We can't stay here, can we? Do you think Ganner had Father killed?"

Moril thought about it. He remembered that, though Ganner had obviously been very pleased to see Lenina, he had not perhaps been entirely surprised. And he did not like it at all. "I don't know. He *could* have done. Only he's a bit feeble to think of it, isn't he?"

"And why not do it years ago, if he felt that bad about Father stealing Mother off him?" said Brid. "But I don't care whether he did or not. I'm not staying here, and that's final!"

"Mother *is* staying," said Moril. "I'm afraid that's final too."

"Then we'll have to do without her," said Brid. "I can cook, and we've got good clothes now. The only thing is, I'm not very good on the hand-organ."

Moril did not feel as if they had come to a decision. It was as if he had known all along that they would leave. "But can we manage?" he said. "Give shows and all without even Dagner?"

"Dagner will have to come too," stated Brid. "He'll have to. He's Father's heir, and he ought to. Besides, he shouldn't stay here even more than us. If it was old days, he'd have to avenge Father."

Moril was dubious. Wherever Brid thought Dagner's duty lay, Moril knew Dagner would want to stay with Lenina. He knew, without knowing how he knew, that Dagner had always been closer to his mother than to Clennen. And how could Dagner take up the singer's trade when he was terrified and nervous at every show? "But, would Dagner do it—on his own? I mean—"

"I know just what you mean," said Brid. "But I can manage Dagner. I can always manage him when there aren't any parents around to interfere."

"Let's go and find him then," said Moril.

Neither of them had seen Dagner for a considerable while. Since they had not the least idea where to start looking, they drifted quite naturally to the stable-yard first, to have a look at Olob and the cart.

Dagner was in the stable-yard, polishing Olob's harness, and Kialan was helping him. Both of them looked a little blank when Moril and Brid came in.

"Do you two haunt this yard, or something?" Kialan said irritably.

Moril decided to take the bull by the horns. "We're taking the cart and leaving," he said. "Are you two coming?" Kialan was clearly astonished and stared at Moril with all the annoyance of someone who cannot believe his ears.

"I've got to go anyway," said Dagner. "Father asked me to take Kialan to Hannart. But there's no need for you two to come."

"Oh yes there is!" said Brid. "One of the men who killed Father is in this house, and if that isn't a reason for going, give me a better one!"

Dagner and Kialan exchanged glances, and Kialan screwed his mouth up. "True?" Dagner said to Moril.

"I saw him," said Moril. "The fair one with queer eyes. But you didn't see them, did—"

"Yes I did," said Dagner. "We were only in the woods. That one was the leader. Kialan, I think that settles it, don't you? We'd better leave at once, as soon as I've said good-bye to Mother."

"Don't be an idiot!" said Moril. "If you tell Mother we're going, she'll tell Ganner. And he's such a big fusspot that he's bound to say it's dangerous and stop us going."

Kialan and Dagner looked at one another again. "He's got a point there, Dagner," Kialan said. "Ganner is an awful old woman. He's bound to come after us anyway. What do you say to waiting until the wedding-feast has started and he's too busy to notice we're missing?"

Dagner pondered anxiously. He looked purple and bent with worry. "No," he said at length.

"No, we daren't. Not if this other fellow's here." He jerked his head to the end of the yard. There was a big old gate in the wall there, bolted and peeling. "We've found out that leads to a back street. You two get those bolts back while I harness Olob, but don't open it till I'm ready."

Kialan helped Dagner pull out the cart and back Olob between its shafts, so they were ready almost as soon as Brid and Moril had done their part. The bolts were very stiff and rusty. Brid wanted to fetch the oil from the cart, but Moril would not let her. "No," he said. "I've an idea to fool Ganner." It took them quite a while, and cost Brid a pinched finger, to waggle the bolts back without.

"Ready," said Dagner. Olob came towards the gate, almost dancing with pleasure at being at the work he was used to. Brid and Moril swung the gate creaking open. Brid went up into the cart, with the easy spring of long practice, and sat down to get her boots off. The cart rumbled through and crunched on the gravel of the lane outside, which was so narrow that Olob for a moment seemed likely to run into the shuttered house opposite. Moril stayed inside the stable-yard and carefully bolted the gate again. It looked, to his satisfaction, as if it had never been opened at all. He took a running jump at it and managed to hook his fingers in the top, where the gate did not quite meet the wall above. From there, he swarmed up on to the thick top of the wall itself. Kialan stood up in the cart to help him jump down.

"Good idea," he said. "Let's hope Ganner wastes a lot of time trying to find out which way we went."

Chapter VI

In the late afternoon, Markind seemed to be deserted. As they clattered northwards through its shuttered, respectable streets, Moril was ready to swear that there was no one around to notice even such a noticeable cart as theirs. Nevertheless, Dagner was as tense as if he were giving a performance. He did not relax even when they were out of Markind. Instead of looking for a main road, he struck into the first small lane that went north and kept turning round uneasily as he drove to see if Ganner was following them.

Olob clattered along with a will, with his ears gaily pricked. The lane, and then the other lanes they took after it, led through apple orchards where the trees were bursting into bloom. The sun was mild and warm. Moril sat smiling sleepily and happily, listening to the familiar beat of Olob's hooves, the wine sloshing about in the great jar behind him, and the blackbirds singing in the appletrees. This was the life! He was sure they could manage, whatever Lenina thought. A cuckoo sang out, cutting across the songs of the blackbirds.

"O—oh!" said Brid. Tears began rolling down her cheeks. "Father said to me—by the lake—he hadn't heard a cuckoo yet this year. And he was sorry he was going to miss it." Her face screwed up and her tears ran faster than ever. "He told me to listen for him, on the way North. And Mother goes and drives straight off to Markind! How could she!"

"Shut up, Brid," said Dagner uncomfortably.

"I shan't! I can't!" cried Brid. "How could she! How could she! Ganner's so stupid. How *could* she!"

"Will you be quiet!" said Dagner. "You don't understand."

"Yes I *do*!" Brid cried. "Ganner and Mother arranged to have Father murdered—that's what happened!"

"Don't talk such blinking nonsense!" Kialan said sharply. "That had nothing to do with either of them."

"How do *you* know?" Brid wept. "Why did she go straight off to Ganner like that?"

"Because she's always wanted to, of course!" said Dagner. "Only she couldn't, because she thought it wasn't honourable. I *told* you you didn't understand," he went on, in an odd, agitated way. "You're too young to notice. But I've seen—oh, enough to know Mother hated living in a cart. She wasn't brought up to it like we are. It was all right while we were in the Earl of Hannart's household— we had a roof over our heads and that wasn't too bad for her—but— I suppose you don't remember."

"Not very well," Brid admitted, sniffing. "I was only three when we left."

"Well, I do," said Dagner. "And Father *would* leave, though he knew Mother didn't want to go. And in the cart she had to bring us up and keep us clean and cook—and she'd never done anything like that in her life till then. And sometimes there

69

was no money at all, and we were always on the move and always—well, there were other things she didn't like Father doing. But Father always got his own way over them. Mother never had a say in anything. She just did the work. Then she saw Ganner again in Derent, after all those years, and she told me it had brought her old life back to her and made her feel terrible. I just don't blame her for going back to what she was used to. You can see Ganner's not going to order her around like Father did."

"Father didn't order her around!" Brid protested. "He even offered to take her back to Ganner."

"Yes, and I thought Mother was really going to call his bluff for a moment then," said Dagner. "He knew darned well Mother wouldn't go, because it wasn't her duty, but he had an anxious moment all the same, didn't he? And then he took good care to point out how much cleverer he was than Ganner."

"That was just his way," said Brid.

"It was all just his way," said Dagner. "Look, Brid, I don't want to pull Father to pieces any more than you do, but in some ways he was—oh, maddening. And if you think about it, you'll see he and Mother weren't at all well matched."

Moril was blinking a little at all this. It was so unlike Dagner to talk so much or so clearly. He marvelled at the way Dagner managed to put into words things Moril had known all his life but not truly noticed till this moment. "Don't you think Mother was fond of Father at all?" he asked dolefully.

"Not in the way we were," said Dagner.

"In that case, why did she run off with him like

that?" Brid asked, triumphantly, as if that clinched the matter.

Dagner looked pensively at a new vista of apple-trees coming into view beyond Olob's ears. "I'm not sure," he said, "but I *think* that cwidder had something to do with it."

Moril swivelled round and cast an apprehensive look at the gleaming belly of the old cwidder, resting in its place in the rack. "Why do you think that?" he asked nervously.

"Something Mother said once," said Dagner. "And Father told you there was power in it, didn't he?"

"There probably is, if it belonged to Osfameron," Kialan observed in a matter-of-fact way.

"Don't be silly! It can't be that old!" Moril protested.

"Osfameron lived not quite two hundred years ago," said Kialan, and he really seemed to know. "He was born the same year as King Labbard died, so it can't be more than that. A cwidder'd surely last as long as that if you took care of it. Why, we've —I've seen one that's four hundred years old— though, mind you, it looks ready to drop apart if you breathed on it."

Moril cast another look, even more apprehensive, at the quiet, prosperous shape of the old cwidder. "It can't be!" he said.

"Well," Dagner said diffidently, "you get used to thinking things like that were only around long ago, but—I'll tell you, Moril—didn't you get the impression you kept Father alive with it this morning?" Moril stared at Dagner with his mouth open. "I thought so," Dagner said, a trifle apologetically. "I've never heard it sound like it did then. And—and Father was dead awfully quickly after you left off, wasn't he?"

Moril was appalled. "Whatever am I going to do with a thing like that!" he almost wailed.

"I don't know. Learn to use it perhaps," said Dagner. "I must say I was glad Father didn't give it to me."

Everyone subsided into thoughtfulness. Brid sniffed wretchedly. Olob clopped steadily on for a mile or so. Then he took a look at the sinking sun and decided to choose them a camping-ground. Dagner dissuaded him. He refused to let Olob turn off the road three times, until Olob got the point and did not try again. They went on and on and on, downhill, uphill, through small valleys, pastures and orchards. The sky died from blue to pink and from pink to purple, and Brid could bear no more.

"Oh, do let's *stop*, Dagner! Today seems to have gone on for about a hundred years!"

"I know," said Dagner. "But I want to get a really good start."

"Do you think Ganner will really follow us?" said Moril. "He ought to be glad we've gone. Then he needn't fuss about roofs and things."

"He's bound to," said Kialan. "A man with a conscience—that's Ganner. He'll probably send some of his hearthmen out tonight and set out himself first thing tomorrow. That's what—I mean, if it had been just Dagner and me, he—"

"Go on. Say it. You think Moril and I shouldn't have come," Brid said bitterly.

"I didn't *say* that!" snapped Kialan.

"Just meant it," said Brid.

"No, he didn't," said Dagner. "Stop being stupid, Brid. The thing is, I left without explaining to Mother, and even if I had explained, she wouldn't have wanted you two to go. So I know she'll ask Ganner to come after us. If he does catch us up, you and Moril will have to go back, I'm afraid."

"Oh *no!*" said Brid, and Moril felt equally mutinous.

"That's why I hope he doesn't catch us," Dagner said. "Because I don't think I could give a show on my own, and I was wondering how on earth I'd manage."

This admission mollified Brid greatly. She refrained from grumbling, although they went on until the light was all but gone. Then Dagner at last permitted Olob to select them a spot on top of a hill. This meant their camp was windy, a fact which Brid bitterly pointed out while they were fumbling around trying to put up the tent in the breezy semi-dark.

"Yes, but we can see people coming," said Dagner.

"And there are thistles. I've just trodden on one," Brid complained.

"Then why on earth don't you put your boots on?" demanded Kialan.

"Oh, I couldn't! I'd spoil them," Brid said, quite shocked.

Kialan roared with laughter, which seemed to restore Brid's frayed temper. She took it quite cheerfully when Moril discovered the only food they had was bread and onions.

"I *knew* we'd need those rabbits," Kialan said dejectedly.

"We all had a good lunch," said Brid.

Moril had the notion of frying the bread and onions together. Unfortunately, it was then so dark that he could not see to fry. The mixture he turned out of the frying-pan was extremely singed, and it was only eaten because everyone was very hungry. Then they settled down to sleep. It seemed to Moril, waking and resettling himself round the winejar during the night, that Kialan and Dagner kept watch, turn and turn about, until dawn broke. Certainly they both looked very jaded in the morning.

Nevertheless, as soon as the sun was up and Olob fed, Dagner had the cart on the move again. They ate the last of the bread as they went. Brid moaned a little, and Dagner promised they would buy more food in the next village they came to.

"What with?" said Brid.

That was a nasty moment. There was no money in the locker where Lenina usually kept it. She must have taken it out in Markind. And none of them had any money in the pockets of their fine new clothes. For a while, it looked as if they would have to give a show before they could eat. Then Brid thought of going through the clothes-locker, turning out pockets. There were a few coins in the pockets of Clennen's scarlet suit, and a further few fell out of Kialan's old good coat when Brid picked it up.

"May we use these? We'll pay you back," she said.

"Of course," said Kialan. "I'd forgotten I'd got any."

When they came to a village, Dagner drew up on the outskirts and sent Brid and Moril shopping, shouting after them at the last minute that there were no more oats for Olob. The rule was that you bought oats first—for where would you be with Olob undernourished?—and they were dear in those parts at that season. Brid and Moril came glumly back with oats, a loaf, half a can of milk, a cold black sausage and a cabbage. Knowing that Dagner would certainly put off giving a performance if he could, Brid prepared to do battle.

"That's all we could afford. If we don't give a show tomorrow, we'll starve," she announced, dumping the meagre purchases in the cart.

"We're going to," Dagner said, to her surprise. "Father said we were to be sure to perform in Neathdale, and I think we'll be there by tomorrow. Have you found it?" he asked Kialan, who was frowning over the map. It was not a good map. Clennen knew Dalemark like the back of his hand and only kept a map for emergencies.

"If this place *is* Cindow, Neathdale's quite a way to the north-west," said Kialan. "Is it worth it? It would be almost as easy to go by the Marshes from here."

"Yes, I've got to go. And he said we'd be bound to get news there," said Dagner. "Let's get going. And," he added, "I suppose we'd better have a bit of a practice this evening."

As Olob went on, Moril, sighing rather, went and fetched the old cwidder. When he had vowed not to play it, he had been thinking of an idle life in Markind—if he had thought of the future at all— but now, whether Dagner played pipes or treble cwidder, and Brid pipes or panhorn, someone was going to have to play tenor to them. That meant

Moril on the big cwidder. And he had always been in awe of it, and never more than now. By way of coming to terms with it, he laid it on his knees and polished it as Clennen had taught him. Brid gave him the note on the panhorn, and he tuned it. And tuned it again. And re-tuned it. As fast as he got a string to the right pitch, it went off again. All he could produce was the moaning twang of slack strings.

"I think the pegs are slipping," he said helplessly.

"Let me have a go," Brid said competently. But she could not get it tuned either.

"Let me look at the pegs," said Kialan. He looked, and seemed fairly knowledgeable, but he could not see anything wrong. He handed it on to Dagner. Dagner, who knew most of all, hitched the reins round his knees and spent half an hour trying to get the cwidder tuned. In the end he was forced to hand it back to Moril in the same state as before.

"Isn't that all we needed!" said Brid. "Perhaps it's in mourning. After all, we all should be, and look at us!"

"Try playing a lament," Kialan said thoughtfully.

"Why?" said Moril. "Anyway, I hate the old songs."

"Any lament," said Dagner. "You played your own treble over the grave, didn't you?"

Moril tried it. He began singing the *Lament for the Earl of Dropwater*, and brought the cwidder in as softly as he could after the first line. The discord was horrible. Brid shuddered. But Dagner took up the song too, and the cwidder seemed almost to follow his lead. The notes came right as Dagner

sang them. To Moril's astonishment and secret
terror, the cwidder was in tune by the end of the
first verse. He sang the chorus, and first Brid, then
Kialan, joined in.

> *This was a man above all other,*
> *Kanart the Earl, Kanart the Earl!*
> *You'll never find his equal, brother.*
> *He was a man above all other.*

The cwidder sang on, as sweetly as it had for
Clennen. Tears poured down Brid's face. Moril
felt tearful too. They sang lustily through the whole
song and, sad though it made them, they felt
heartened too. The oddest effect was on Olob. His
pace dropped to a slow, rhythmic walk, and he went
for all the world as if the cart was a hearse.

"Put it away," said Dagner, "or we'll never get to
Neathdale."

Moril put the alarming cwidder carefully back
and they made better progress. As before, Dagner
would not let Olob stop at the usual time, or in the
usual kind of place. A little before sunset, he took
Olob right off the road into a high, lonely field full
of big stones, where they could see a good way in
most directions.

"There hasn't been a sign of Ganner!" Moril
protested.

"Well, there won't be, until we see him arriving,
will there?" said Kialan.

They demolished the sausage and held their
practice. To Moril's relief, the big cwidder now
behaved perfectly. But there were other difficulties.
Without Clennen or Lenina, they found they could
not do half the songs in the way they were used to.

They had to work everything out afresh. And Dagner did not in any way take Clennen's place. He refused to do more than a third of the singing, and that was the only thing he was firm about. Otherwise, he simply made suggestions, and he was quite ready to be overruled by Brid or Moril. The younger two felt lost. They were used to Clennen's kind but entirely firm way of telling them exactly what to do. Sometimes they were annoyed, and several times they were tempted to get very silly. It was only the grim thought that their next meal depended on this practice that kept them from breaking into loud arguments or louder laughter. Moril felt he had never truly missed Clennen till then.

Yet, in the middle of thinking that, he remembered what Dagner had said about Clennen always having his own way. It occurred to him to wonder if Clennen had not, in fact, kept them all a little too dependent on him. Maybe this was why it seemed so hard to manage without him.

While they practised, Kialan lay full length on a rock above them, listening, and also, Moril suspected, acting as lookout. This elaborate caution began to irritate Moril. After all, it was Moril and Brid who stood to lose if Ganner found them, not Dagner and Kialan. In the morning, he was exasperated to see that they had been on watch again. Both of them looked tired out.

Brid was furious. "How on earth do you think you're going to give a performance, Dagner, if you can hardly keep your eyes open? I've never known you so silly! We *depend* on you!"

"All right," Dagner said wearily. "You drive and

I'll have a sleep in the cart. But wake me if—if—"

"If *what*?" snapped Brid.

"If anything happens," said Dagner and lay down beside the winejar with a groan. Kialan flopped down on the other side of the jar, and both of them fell asleep before Olob had the cart in motion.

It was left to Brid and Moril to find the way to Neathdale. They did it, too, half cross and half proud of themselves. The map did not help much. They were forced to follow their noses across country, turning into any road that seemed to go north-west and hoping for the best. Once they arrived in a farmyard and had to back out of it, pursued by the barking of dogs and the squalling of hens and roosters. Kialan and Dagner did not even stir. "Stupid fools," said Brid. They were still asleep when the cart came out on a rise above Neathdale.

"We did it!" said Moril.

"Unless Olob knew the way," Brid said, trying to be fair. "But I don't think even he can have come to it this way before."

Neathdale was a big cheerful-looking town lying across the main road north to Flennpass, in the last level ground before the Uplands. They could look across even its tallest buildings from where they were to where the South Dales mounted like stairs to the Mark Wood plateau.

"Say four days, and we'll be in the North," Moril said yearningly.

"Four days," said Brid promptly.

The scuffle that followed on the driving-seat woke Dagner and Kialan at last. "What's the matter? What's going on?"

"Nothing. Only Neathdale," said Brid. Dagner's sleepy face at once became pinched and tense and mauvish. Brid set herself to soothe him. "We always used to get good takings here," she said. "There must be hundreds of people who remember us and know Father. I'm going to do the talking, mind, and I shall talk about Father and say who we are—though they can read that on the cart anyway."

"The cart ought to be repainted with Dagner's name," Moril observed. He did not think Brid was soothing Dagner in the slightest, but he did not mind helping.

"You'd hardly get the name on," Brid said brightly. "Dastgandlen down one side and Handagner up the other, I suppose."

"Isn't Neathdale the seat of Earl Tholian?" Kialan asked, tactlessly cutting through the soothing.

"Not really. His place is outside a bit, over to the east," Dagner said. He pointed with a hand that shook noticeably. A great white house was just visible, among trees, on the other side of Neathdale.

"Blast you, Kialan!" said Brid. Kialan looked at her in surprise. "Oh, it doesn't matter," said Brid. "Just if this show goes wrong, I'll blame you. Dagner, I think we'd better put on our glad-rags now."

"No," said Dagner.

"What do you mean?" said Brid.

"Just No," said Dagner. "We'll give the show as we are. We're quite respectable."

"Yes, but we always change," Brid protested. "It gives you a feel."

"That was Father's idea," said Dagner. "And he was right in a way. It went with his style to come rolling in, singing and glittering. He could live up to it. But if I go in dressed in tinsel and singing my head off, people are just going to laugh."

"You think that because you're nervous," Brid said persuasively. "You'll feel better once you're changed."

"No I won't," said Dagner. "I'll feel ten times worse. Brid, I just haven't got Father's personality, and I can't do the same things. I'll have to do them my way, or not at all. See?"

Brid, by this time, was near tears. "Do you mean you're not going to give a show at all then?"

"Not Father's kind," said Dagner, "because I can't. We'll give a show all right, because we'll starve if we don't, and you can introduce us and explain what's happened, and maybe it'll be all right. But if I find you boasting and ranting about us—that goes for you too, Moril—I'll stop. We'll just have to be plain, because we're not Father."

Brid sighed heavily. "All right. But I'm going to put my boots on, anyway. I need a feel." She brightened a little. "I've always hated the colour of your suit, Moril. You look nicer like that."

"Thank you," Moril said politely. Dagner had suddenly brought it home to him that, for the first time in their lives, they were about to give a show entirely on their own. He had never, as far as he knew, been nervous before. Now he was. As Brid drove downhill towards Neathdale, Moril sat clutching the big cwidder with hands that were icy cold and sweating at once, and it would have been hard to say whether he or Dagner was the more nervous. The houses came nearer. Quite desperate, Moril laid his cheek against the smooth wood of the cwidder. "Oh please help me!" he whispered to it. "I'll never manage. I can't!"

"Can you stop a moment?" said Kialan.

Brid drew up. Kialan immediately swung down from the cart to the road. Brid looked at him sombrely. "Now you're going to give us that about not being interested in our shows, aren't you? Well, don't. I won't believe you. I've seen you listening to every show we've given."

Kialan looked up at Brid's stormy face and seemed nonplussed. Then he laughed. "All right. I won't give you that. But I'm going to meet you on the other side of Neathdale all the same. See you." He set off at a good swinging pace towards the town, with his hands in his pockets, whistling *Jolly Holanders*.

"I give up!" said Brid. But both her brothers were too nervous to reply.

Chapter VII

The main square at Neathdale was always busy. It was not very large, but it had a handsome fountain in the middle and four inns on three of its sides. There was also a corn-exchange and two guildhalls, which added to the coming and going. The fourth side was occupied by the grey frowning block of the jail. When Brid drove the cart into the square, it seemed busier even than they had remembered. It was packed with people. The reason they saw, as Olob patiently shouldered his way towards the fountain, was that there had been a public hanging that morning. The gallows was still there, outside the jail, and so was the hanged man. A number of people outside the inns were raising tankards jeeringly in his direction.

The dangling figure made them all feel sick, although it meant a good crowd. Dagner turned green. Moril clutched his cwidder hard and swallowed. Brid could not resist leaning down and asking the nearest person who it was who had been hanged.

"Friend of the Porter's," was the cheerful reply. It was a cheerful whiskery man Brid had chosen to ask, and he looked as if he had enjoyed every second of the hanging. "Some say he *was* the Porter," he added, "but you can't tell. He wouldn't admit to anything. Taken up last week, he was, on the new Earl's orders."

"Oh, is there a new Earl?" Brid said blankly, trying to keep her eyes from the swinging criminal.

"Sure," said the man. "Old Tholian died more than a month back. The new Earl's the grandson. Got a real nose for the Porter and his like, he has. Good luck to him too!"

"Oh, yes. Very good luck," Brid said hurriedly, terrified of being arrested for disloyalty to the new Earl.

"Leave off, Brid, and let's get started," Dagner said irritably.

Brid smiled rather falsely at the whiskery man and hitched up the reins so that Olob knew to stand still. Then she blew a blast on the panhorn for attention. When sufficient people had turned their way, she stood up and spoke. Moril marvelled at how cool she was. But Brid was like Clennen that way. An audience was meat and drink to her.

"Ladies and gentlemen," she called, "please come and listen. You see the cart I'm standing in? Many of you will know it quite well. If you do, you'll know it belongs to Clennen the Singer. You'll have seen it coming through Neathdale, year after year, on its way north. Most of you will know Clennen the Singer—"

She had aroused people's interest by then. Moril heard someone say, "It's Clennen the Singer."

"No it isn't," said someone else. "Who's the pretty little lass?"

"Where's Clennen, then? It isn't Clennen," said other people. Finally, someone was puzzled enough to call out, "Where is Clennen, lass? Isn't he with you?"

"I'll tell you," said Brid. "I'll tell you all." Then she stopped and simply stood there, upright and conspicuous in her cherry dress. Moril could see she was trying not to cry. But he could also see she was making it plain to the crowd that she was trying not to cry. He marvelled at the way she could use real feelings for what was in fact a show. He knew he could not have done it.

Brid stood there silent long enough for murmurs of interest to gather and grow, but not long enough for them to die away. Then she said: "I'll tell you. Clennen—my father—was killed two days ago." And she stood silent again, struggling with tears, listening attentively to murmurs of sympathy. "He was killed before our eyes," she said. At the height of a loud murmur, she came in again, loudly, but in such a calm way that Moril and most of the people present thought she was speaking quietly. They hushed to hear her. "We are the children of Clennen the Singer—Brid, Moril and Dastgandlen Handagner—and we're doing our best to carry on without him. I hope you'll spare time to listen to us. We know our show will not be the same without Clennen, but—but we'll try to please you. We hope you'll forgive any faults in—in memory of my father."

She got a round of applause for that. "Put your hat out, then, and let's hear you!" someone shouted. Brid, with tears running down her cheeks, picked up the hat she had ready and tossed it on the ground. Several people put money into it at once, out of pure sympathy for them. Brid could not help feeling pleased with herself. She had made a considerable effect without boasting once—in fact, she had done the opposite, which, she thought, ought to please Dagner.

Though Dagner was far too nervous to show any pleasure at all, Brid knew he was not displeased, because he left her to do all the announcing. That meant that Brid could more or less choose what they sang. She did her best to put together the things they had practised in the order she thought would be most impressive. She began them with general favourites. Moril felt terrible. Without the deep rolling voice of Clennen, they sounded to him thin and strange, and they lacked the body Lenina usually gave them on the hand-organ. Moril began to feel they had nothing to offer the crowd, except perhaps some well-trained playing on cwidder and panhorn.

Brid felt much the same. To encourage them, she announced that they would now play, in trio, the *Seven Marches*. That was one thing she was sure they could do well. And they did. The most successful part was when Dagner, on the spur of the moment, signalled to Brid to play soft during the *Fourth March*, and played his treble cwidder in double time against Moril's slow and mellow tenor. They looked at one another while they were doing it. Moril knew they were neither of them exactly enjoying it, but they were both by then desperate for some applause from the silent crowd, and they had the dour kind of satisfaction of knowing they were giving an exhibition of real skill. They were rewarded by a burst of clapping and a little shower of coins falling into the hat.

Then they did Clennen's *Cuckoo Song*, which always made people laugh. After that Brid, feeling that the sooner Dagner got his part over, the better he would be for the rest of the show, announced that Dagner would now sing some of his own songs.

Brid was glad she had said "some". Dagner was so nervous that he only managed three. If she had not said "some", it was probable that he would only have sung one. Moril was disappointed and Brid exasperated, and it was altogether a pity, because the crowd liked Dagner's songs. *The colour in your head* went down particularly well. Brid could tell he had the crowd's sympathy. They thought of him as bravely following in Clennen's footsteps and wanted to encourage him. But Dagner was mauve and shaking and he stopped.

Crossly, Brid took the centre of the cart and sang herself. Moril, without being told, came to her aid on the cwidder, while Dagner gasped to himself in the background. Brid did well. An audience always helped her. She sang a number of ballads—though she was forced to avoid *The hanging of Filli Ray*, which she did best, because of the corpse dangling on the gallows behind the crowd. Her success was undoubtedly the patter song, *Cow-Calling*, which she did instead of *Filli Ray*. Brid always enjoyed it. You started with a sort of yodelling cry, to the whole herd, then you called the cows one by one, and each verse you added a new one.

Red cow, red cow, my lord's thoroughbred cow,
Brown cow, brown cow, the woman in the town's cow,

Brid sang, and no one looking at her could have realised that she was frantically wondering what else she could put into their unusually short show before her voice gave out. At *Old cow, old cow,* inspiration came. Brid bowed at the end of the song. Coins clattered into the hat.

"Now, ladies and gentlemen, my brother Moril will sing four songs of Osfameron."

Moril gulped and glared at Brid. He had never performed any of the old songs in public before. But Brid had gone and announced him, so he was forced to take the centre of the cart, with his wet hands shaking on the cwidder. To make matters worse, he suddenly met Kialan's eye. Kialan was standing near the fountain, looking cool, attentive, and slightly critical. From where Moril stood, the hanged man on the gallows appeared to be dangling over Kialan's head. Moril took his eyes off both of them and began to play. He knew he was going to make wretched work of it.

For a short while, he could attend to nothing but the queer fingering and the odd, old-fashioned rhythms. Then his tension abated a little, and he was surprised to discover that his performance was pleasing him. As Moril's voice was naturally high, he did not need to sound cracked and strained, the way Clennen did. And, not being yet expert and not anyway liking the noise the old fingering made, he found he had been unconsciously modifying it, into a style which was not old, nor new, but different. Osfameron's jerky rhythms became smoother, and Moril felt that, if he could have spared time to attend to them, he might almost have understood the words:

> *The Adon's hall was open. Through it*
> *Swallows darted. The soul flies through life.*

Osfameron in his mind's eye knew it.
The bird's life is not the man's life.

Osfameron walked in the eye
Of his mind. The blackbird flew there.
He would not let the blackbird's song go by.
His mind's life can keep the bird there.

It sounded good to Moril. And it was his own doing, he was positive, and not the cwidder's. When he had finished, however, there was silence in the square. The crowd had never heard the old songs done that way and did not know what to think. Kialan made up their minds for them by clapping loudly. Other people clapped. Then came a burst of applause which made Moril feel ashamed of himself—he was only a learner, after all—and more coins went into the hat.

The applause seemed to worry Olob. From then on, he became restive. He tossed his head, he stamped, he tried to go forward, and he threatened to back. Brid pulled him up, and he backed in earnest, throwing Moril into Dagner. Brid had to take the reins up again, which put her half out of action. Seeing this, Dagner pulled himself together and led into some songs with rousing choruses, hoping the crowd would join in. He had little luck. People were in the mood for listening. But they had come to the end of all they had practised, so Dagner was forced to go on to *Jolly Holanders* and finish.

Olob was still behaving like a colt, so Moril got down and went to his head. The crowd shifted away from the cart. Moril heard Brid say to Dagner, "Shall I go shopping? I know what to get," and the hat chinking.

"No, I'll go," said Dagner. He still seemed nervous, although the show was over. He took the hat and climbed down from the cart. Almost at once, several men that Moril recognised as friends of Clennen's came up and crowded round Dagner.

"What's this, Dagner? What's this about Clennen?"

The upshot was that Dagner went off to have a drink with them, taking the hat. Moril did not see which inn they went to because he found himself being talked to by a kindly man just then. This man first gave Moril a pie, then told him—in a fatherly way—that he had sung the old songs all wrong, and things were going to the dogs if people could take those kind of liberties.

Moril took a leaf out of Dagner's book. "Yes, but I can't do it like my father did," he said with his mouth full. He was extremely grateful for the pie, or he would have told the man his real opinion of the old songs.

When the man had gone, muttering that he didn't know what the young were coming to, Moril remembered that Brid would be a prey to murmuring gentlemen. He looked up at the cart, wondering what he would do if she was. There was—or had been—a murmuring gentleman. Brid was glaring at him like a tiger, and the gentleman was retreating, very red in the face. "I do hope Dagner remembers the shopping," Brid said to Moril, pretending the gentleman had never existed.

So did Moril. They waited, and waited, Moril at Olob's restive head and Brid in the cart, for well over an hour. Moril saw Kialan at intervals, hanging about in the square, evidently waiting too. But

Kialan made no attempt to come near them. Moril rather irritably wondered why not.

Olob tossed his head furiously. Brid said, "There's Dagner!" Moril saw Dagner hurrying back across the square with the empty hat rolled up in one hand. "Where's the shopping?" Brid wondered. Dagner waved cheerfully and came hurrying on. He had almost reached the cart, when two large men advanced, quietly and purposefully, on either side of Dagner. One took Dagner's shoulder in a large hand.

"What—?" said Dagner, trying to shake free.

"You're under arrest, in the Earl's name," said the man. "Come on quietly and don't make any trouble now."

For a moment, Moril had another glimpse of Kialan, looking absolutely horrified, in the crowd beyond the fountain. The people near, seeing someone being arrested, drifted quickly away from around the cart. Kialan seemed to get lost in a moving group and was gone the next second. Moril stood by Olob's head in an empty space, quite irrationally angry with Kialan. Not that anyone could do anything if the Earl took it into his head to have Dagner arrested, but even Kialan would have been better than no one. He looked despairingly at Dagner. Dagner had only time for one hopeless look back before the two men led him away across the square towards the jail. The crowd hurried away from all three—as if Dagner had a disease, Moril thought angrily. He wished Dagner would walk upright, instead of going bent and guilty-looking.

"I've never been so furious in my life!" said Brid. "Never! Of all the unjust—" She stopped, and looked uneasily round the empty space by the fountain, realising she was on the way to getting herself arrested too.

The two men vanished with Dagner inside the frowning jail. Moril had never felt more lonely. "I've just realised," he said. "We didn't have a licence to sing, did we?"

"We're entitled to operate on Father's for six months," said Brid. "Father told me, and I *know* that's the law. I hope Dagner remembers. They can't *do* this! They're just trying—"

A man approached across the empty space, rather grudgingly, carrying what looked like a sack of oats. He stopped some way off the cart. "Your brother ordered this," he said. "Do I take it away again?"

"You'll do no such thing!" Brid said haughtily. "It's paid for—that I do know. Put it in the cart."

"Please yourself," said the man unpleasantly. He dumped the sack on the flagstones and went away.

That was nasty, somehow. Moril saw that everyone was going to avoid them now. Angrily, he supposed that Kialan had deserted them in the same way. He left Olob, who seemed to be quietening down, and dragged the sack over to the cart. "What shall we *do*, Brid?"

"Do?" said Brid, more furious than ever. "I'll tell you what to do. I'll have to stay here, in case Dagner ordered anything else, but you're to go over to the jail at *once* and ask to see Dagner. Go on. Tell them he's related to the Earl. Say Mother's Tholian's niece. Make a fuss. Ask them to send for Ganner. Make it quite clear that we're well-connected. And when you see Dagner, tell him to do the same. Go on. They're just trying to frighten us into paying for another licence, I know they are!"

Obediently, Moril scurried off across the square. He was so shaken that he could think of nothing else to do, even though he knew in his heart that it was no good. In the South, when they arrested people, even for small offences, it took more than a boy talking about noble relatives to get them out of prison. At the least, it took a lot of money. And, as they had not got a lot of money, the doors of the jail could well have closed on Dagner for good. Moril wished Ganner had found them, after all. By the time he reached the cold archway into the jail, he was heartily wishing they had never left Markind.

"Please," he said to the man on duty there, "I want to see my brother."

The man looked down at him, not unkindly. "Clennen the Singer's son?" Moril nodded. "And how old are you, lad?" asked the man.

"Eleven," said Moril.

"Eleven, are you?" said the man. "They don't hang your kind till they're fifteen, you know, so you're lucky." Moril thought this was meant to be a joke, and smiled politely. "Look, lad," said the man. "Take some good advice. Get in that cart of yours and drive off. You won't do any good here."

Moril looked up at him in helpless irritation. "But—"

"Be off!" said the man, urgently. Footsteps were coming through the dark passage behind him. Moril could see the man meant kindly, but he did not move. He waited to see if the person coming would let him see Dagner.

The man who came was one of the two who had arrested Dagner. He glanced at Moril, without seeming very interested. Then he looked again—sharply. "That's another of them, isn't it?"

"Yes, sir," said the man at the gate, and he gave Moril a reproachful look, as much as to say, "Now see what you've done."

"Come with me, lad," said the other man. Moril, with his stomach hopping as it had never done before, even before this last show, followed him into the dark passageway, through a dismal courtyard and up some stone stairs. They went into a blank room with yellow walls and a bench by one of the walls, where the man told him to sit and wait. Then he went out and locked the door.

Moril sat on the bench for some time, feeling terrible. He wondered if he was arrested too. It looked like it. He tried to see out of the window, but it was high up and barred. He dragged the bench over to it, but he still could not see much except grey walls. There was no hope of wriggling out between the bars. He dragged the bench back to its original position and sat on it again.

Then the most dreadful part began. He could not bear being shut between walls. He was hot. He was trapped. The room seemed to get smaller every second and the ceiling seemed to be moving down on him. He thought he would have to scream. He nearly did scream, when a fortunate stain on the wall opposite caught his attention. It was almost the shape of the mountains between Dropwater and Hannart.

Moril thankfully escaped into a dream. He imagined snow-capped mountains and forgot he was too hot. He imagined wide valleys and the sky overhead, and the small room became easier to bear. He thought of the old green roads of the North and of Osfameron and the Adon walking along them. He became Osfameron himself. He and his friend the Adon made their way to imaginary Hannart. On the mountain, they were ambushed by enemies and fought their way clear. Then they went down into Hannart and strolled under the rowan trees outside the old grey castle, composing a song of victory together.

The door opened and another man told Moril to come along now, quickly.

Moril came back to the present with a jump. He was scared and vibrating and small. He was aware of every stone and stain in that oppressive room, of the grain in the wood of the door, and the dirt in the fingernails of the man's hand holding it open. He even knew there were six hairs in the mole on the man's nose. As he got up, he suddenly remembered Clennen by the lake, saying, "You're in two halves at present". And he wondered if this was what Clennen had meant.

The man ushered him into a large, imposing room, with a heavy old table at one end. An elderly man sat behind the table, with a younger one who was taking notes. Moril could see by the gold chain round the elderly one's neck that he was a Justice.

"Stand in front of the table and answer clearly," said the younger man, pausing in his writing and pointing his pen at Moril.

Moril did as he was told, still vibrating. He knew every bulge in the rather pointless carving on the wall above the Justice. He could tell how many wrinkles there were in the forehead of the Justice—fifteen yellowish folds.

The Justice wrinkled these folds up and looked at Moril. "Full name?"

"Osfameron Tanamoril Clennensson," said Moril. "I'd like to see my brother, please."

"Quite a mouthful," remarked the Justice, while the other man wrote it down. "Osfameron?"

"He's my ancestor," said Moril. Seeing that the yellow folds of the Justice were lifted towards him with slight interest, he explained, "I was called after him. And could I see Dagner, please?" The yellow folds drew closer together. "My brother," Moril said patiently.

"Your brother?" said the Justice. The other man passed him a sheaf of papers, and he drew the folds of his forehead together over them until it looked like smocking. "Some other mouthful down here," he said.

Moril, with a little wobble to his stomach, realised the papers must be Dagner's answers to the questions they had asked him. He wondered what Dagner had said and wished he knew. For, if he gave different answers from Dagner's, the Justice might well convict Dagner of all sorts of things he had never done. "We call him Dagner for short," he explained carefully. "And I'd like to see him, please."

"You can see him presently, if you answer my questions truthfully," said the Justice. "You come of a family of singers, is that true?"

"Yes," said Moril.

"And you travelled with your father, giving shows?"

96

"Yes," said Moril.

"How long have you been doing that?"

"All my life," said Moril.

"Which is how long?"

"Eleven years," said Moril.

The younger man leant over. "The elder boy said ten years."

The Justice smocked his forehead at Moril, calculating how old he was. He looked weary and shrewd, and Moril was just a doubtful fact to him. Moril saw that to follow Brid's advice and talk of being related to the Earl and to Ganner would do no good, simply no good at all. He knew Brid would have done it. But he was not going to try.

"I was a baby when we started," he explained.

"From Hannart?" said the Justice sharply.

"Yes, but I don't remember," Moril said, knowing well enough that if he admitted to his true feelings about Hannart here, he could convict both himself and Dagner. "My father said he had a quarrel with Earl Keril."

They checked that off against Dagner's answers, and it seemed to be right, to Moril's relief. But they seemed dissatisfied, and they became more dissatisfied as the questions went on.

"Where did you last perform before Neathdale?"

Moril thought. It seemed very long ago. Fledden? Yes, because that was the last place before they were in the Markind lordship and stopped performing. That was where Lenina had mended Kialan's coat. "Fledden," he said.

"Who did your brother talk to in Fledden?"

"Nobody," said Moril. He remembered particularly, because no girls had come up to Dagner for once, and he had talked to Dagner himself.

"But you weren't with him every moment you were in Fledden, were you?" said the younger man.

"Yes, I was," said Moril. "We were all in the cart, you see. Father always made us stay in the cart together in towns."

"Always?" said the Justice, smocking his folds severely. "You don't mean to tell me your brother never went off on his own."

Moril realised he could convict Dagner of poaching rabbits unless he was careful. "No, never," he said. "Dagner's not interested in anything much except making up songs." And, to divert attention from the idea of poaching, he added, "Dagner hasn't done anything you could arrest him for—and our licence is in order, honestly."

The Justice sighed irritably. "I'm not concerned with your licence, boy. Your brother has been arrested for passing illegal information—"

"*What!*" said Moril.

"—and I want to know where he got it," said the Justice. "That surprises you?"

"I should just say it does!" said Moril. "He couldn't have done! You must have made a mistake."

"Our agents are very reliable," said the Justice. "What makes you think it's a mistake?"

"Because Dagner wouldn't. He's just not interested. He's only interested in making songs. Besides, there's nowhere he *could* have got information," Moril said frantically.

"That sort of assertion is not at all helpful," said the Justice. "I fancy both you brothers are concealing something. You say you last performed in Fledden. That must have been a week ago. Where have you been since?"

"Markind," said Moril, wondering why on earth Dagner had not mentioned it. "Then we came here by Cindow."

The Justice and the younger man looked at one another, and seemed incredulous. It was clear that they thought Markind the last place where anyone could obtain illegal information. Moril took heart a little. "Why Markind?" snapped the younger man.

"My father was killed," Moril explained, his voice wobbling a little.

"We know. At Medmere. Why did you go to Markind?" said the younger man.

"My mother went to marry Ganner," said Moril.

"*Ganner!*" they both exclaimed and both looked at Moril in flat disbelief. "Ganner is Lord of Markind," the Justice said, as if he thought Moril did not know.

"I know," said Moril. "Mother was betrothed to him before she married Father, and she went back there."

"Very likely," the Justice said cynically. "In that case, why did you and your brother leave?"

Angry tears came into Moril's eyes. "Because I saw one of the men who killed Father there, if you must know! And if you don't believe me, ask Ganner!"

"I most certainly shall," said the Justice. The other man murmured something to him, and they looked at one another, the wrinkles of the Justice smocked into a tight yellow bunch. Moril saw Brid had been right after all to tell him to mention

Ganner. But, like Brid, the Justice had jumped to the conclusion that Ganner had had Clennen killed, and the younger man was wagging his eyebrows at him to warn him that Ganner was far too important to be accused. The Justice showed himself neither very nice nor very just by giving a cynical little laugh, smiling and shrugging. Moril supposed he should be glad, if, as Kialan had said, Ganner really had nothing to do with Clennen's death. Then the Justice turned to Moril again and Moril saw, sadly and rather bitterly, that there was one law for Ganner and quite another for himself and Dagner. "Did your brother talk to any strangers in Markind?"

"No," said Moril. "Only Ganner's household."

"Then who did he talk to between Markind and here?"

"Only us," said Moril.

"Listen, my boy," said the Justice, "you're not being very helpful, are you? Perhaps it will jog your memory if I remind you that your brother's crime is one for which he will be hanged in due course. Therefore, I can put you in prison for withholding information."

Moril felt sick. "I *am* being helpful," he said. "I've *told* you it's a mistake. But if you're only going to believe me if I tell you Dagner's guilty, then it's no use asking me questions. Because he didn't do it!"

The younger man half stood up, looking savage. Moril blinked and waited for them to hit him, or clap him in a cell, or both. But they did neither. The younger man, after a dreadful pause, told Moril coldly to go and sit down at the other end of the long room. Moril did so. He sat on a hard shiny stool near the door and watched the two conferring together in low voices. There were footsteps beyond the door, so that he was unable to hear anything that was said, though he thought he caught Ganner's name more than once. Then they called him back to the table.

"We're going to let you go, boy," said the younger one. "We've come to the conclusion you know nothing about this matter."

"Thank you," said Moril. "Can I see my brother now?"

The younger man glared at him and was obviously going to refuse. But the Justice said irritably, "Oh, very well, very well. I said you should if you answered my questions. I wouldn't like you to go away thinking we're unjust here."

Moril thought Brid would have made the obvious answer to this. He held his tongue, with a bit of an effort.

Chapter VIII

The man who had fetched Moril before came back. He took Moril downstairs to a great gloomy room with guards at the door. In the middle of this room were two rows of benches about three feet apart. People were sitting facing one another at intervals along these benches. Those on the further bench were all prisoners. Moril could see they were, because they all had a dingy, sullen, dejected look and held their heads hunched forward. He had once seen a dancing bear with the same look. And the people on the nearer bench were plainly visitors, from not having that look, and being brisker and more nervous. There seemed to be guards everywhere, standing about in a bored way, and the nervous looks of the visitors were mostly directed at the guards. The room rang and whispered with shuffling feet and sad conversations.

The man told Moril to sit on the nearest bench. After a while, two guards led Dagner through a door at the other end. Dagner had the same dingy, dejected look already. He looked unexpectedly small between the guards. Moril was sure he remembered him bigger.

They sat Dagner down on the bench opposite Moril. "You can have ten minutes," they told

Moril. Then they left them to talk. Moril swallowed and could not think what to say.

"Just a moment," said Dagner. "Look at the room behind me, will you, and tell me if there's anyone you think can hear what we say."

Moril looked. The nearest guard was a good way off, talking to another. "No. They're two cart-lengths away at least." He was about to turn round and see if there was anyone behind him.

"Don't move, you fool!" said Dagner. "I can see it's all right behind you."

"Then that's all right," said Moril. "I saw the Justice and I told them it's all a mistake. They can't really think you were passing information, can they? It's just not true."

"Yes it is," said Dagner. "I did."

Moril stared at him.

"Father asked me to," Dagner explained. "I had to give a message and some money to one of our men here. I didn't manage very well," he said sadly. "I wasn't sure—anyway, I think the one I gave it to must have been the spy. And when I think how relieved I was once I'd got rid of them, I—well, it's no use thinking of that, I suppose."

"But Dagner!" Moril said, quite horrified. "They'll hang you for that!"

"You don't think I don't know that, do you?" Dagner said irritably. "Is there still no one near?"

"No," said Moril. "Dagner, it isn't true, is it? You're joking."

"I'm not joking," said Dagner. "If you don't believe me, take a look at that winejar—unless they've searched the cart by now. But that's not important. What *is* important is that you've got to get Kialan into the North. You and Brid just have to go on and get him to Hannart if you can. Can you do that, Moril?"

"I suppose so," said Moril. "But I think he sloped off when they arrested you."

"No, he didn't," said Dagner. "He'll be waiting outside Neathdale, like he said."

"If you think so—Dagner, *why* is it so important?"

"Ask Kialan," said Dagner, with his eyes on someone behind Moril. "I ordered some flour and some more oats," he went on, rather artificially. "And there was a friend of Father's letting me have a side of bacon cheap. And onions. You can get bread on the way."

"And eggs," agreed Moril. "And I'll polish your cwidder for you, I promise."

"You needn't bother," said Dagner. "Right, he's gone. Now, listen. There are two things I want you to tell Kialan. One is that Henda *has* asked a ransom for him—"

"Ransom for Kialan?" said Moril. "But he's—"

"Never mind. Just tell him," said Dagner. "And the other thing is far more important. Earl Tholian is gathering an army and—"

"Tholian? He's dead," Moril objected, and he had a muddled and upsetting notion of an army of ghosts.

"This is the new Earl. He's called Tholian too. Don't keep interrupting. There's someone on his way over behind you," said Dagner. "The point is that nobody in the North knows, and there's nobody going through but you and Kialan. Have you got those two things?"

"Ransom and Tholian," said Moril. "There's somebody coming behind *you* now."

The guards behind Dagner came right up to him. "Come on. Time's up."

"We haven't had anything like ten minutes," Moril pointed out.

"Too bad. The Justice wants to see him. On your feet, fellow," said the guard.

Dagner got up and climbed back over the bench. He made Moril a face as he was marched off, which Moril thought was intended for a smile. Moril himself, feeling utterly crushed, wandered to the door and was shown briskly through to the entrance again.

"You're out again, are you?" said the man on duty. "You've been lucky."

Moril had not the heart to reply. He did not think he was lucky, particularly as the first thing that met his eyes outside was the two dangling feet of the hanged man.

Beyond the dangling feet, Brid was sitting in the cart looking haughty and impatient. The cart was still in a clear space, and the sack of oats had been joined by a number of other sacks and bundles, all of them too heavy for Brid to lift by herself.

"Where have you *been*?" she demanded, as soon as Moril was near enough. "I thought you were never coming back! What's the matter? You look like a jug of spilt milk."

Moril was feeling so lost and peculiar that all he could do was to go to Olob. He put his arms round Olob's neck and rubbed his forehead on Olob's nose.

"Well, tell me!" said Brid. "Have you seen Dagner?"

"Yes," said Moril.

"Did you tell him to say what I told you?"

"No," said Moril.

"Why *not*? Moril, I shall hit you in a moment, if you don't tell me sensibly what happened!"

"I can't," said Moril. "Not here."

"Why *not*?" Brid almost shouted.

Moril realised that he must stop her attracting attention to them. "Please, Brid. Shut up," he said, looking at her as meaningly as he could from beside Olob's nose. "Let's get these sacks loaded and get on."

Brid began to see that something terrible might have happened. "Without Dagner?" she said, in a more subdued voice. Moril nodded, tore himself away from warm, soft, friendly Olob, and began to heave at the nearest sack. Brid came down and joined him. "Moril, for goodness sake!" she whispered angrily. "It can't be that bad! You're behaving as if they're going to *hang* Dagner."

"They are," said Moril.

Brid went white, but she did not really believe him. "Oh no!" she said. "Not on top of everything! Why?"

"Get these things in and I'll tell you when we're moving," Moril said.

They loaded the cart and Brid drove out of the square. When they came into the cobbled streets, where the cart made sufficient clatter to cover up whispers, Moril told Brid what had happened. It turned Brid so sick and weak that had Olob been that kind of horse, he could easily have got out of control.

"I can't believe it!" she kept saying.

She was still saying it when, half a mile out of Neathdale, Kialan pushed his way out of a hedge and came to join them. When he first looked at them, he was smiling, as if he were relieved. Then he saw there were only two of them, and his smile vanished. He looked along the cart to make sure Dagner was not there, and then at their faces. When he climbed up to join them, his brown face was tired and yellowish. "What happened?" he said. "Better drive on."

"Moril says they're going to hang Dagner for passing information," said Brid. "He says Father told Dagner to do it. And I can't believe it! I just can't believe it!"

"Oh," said Kialan. "They got him for that, did they? I thought that was too much of a risk on top of everything else."

"You're mighty cool, aren't you?" said Brid. "But I suppose Dagner's not your brother!"

There was a pause, in which Kialan tried to control his feelings. But his natural outspokenness won. "All right," he said. "So he's not my brother. So you think I don't know how you feel. You just thank your stars, my girl, that you don't have to stand there and watch them hang Dagner, like I had to with *my* brother!" Brid and Moril turned round in the driving-seat to stare at Kialan. But they turned back, because there were large, angry tears running past Kialan's high-bridged nose, and more tears filling and reddening his light blue eyes. "I always thought the world of Dagner, anyway," he said. "I remembered him quite well from when we were small."

There was silence, except for horse and cart noises. Brid encouraged Olob to make the best speed he could up the first steep hill to the Uplands. It was horrible to be urging Olob away from

107

Dagner. There were tears in Brid's eyes too.

"Why did they hang your brother?" Moril asked at length.

"No reason," Kialan said angrily. "It was Tholian's idea—that pale-eyed murdering swine who killed your father—but I didn't hear Hadd or Henda or any of the others making much objection. They just had us put on trial first, to make it seem respectable. And then it came out that I was only fourteen—"

"Oh! I thought you were older!" said Brid.

"People do," said Kialan. "But I was fourteen in March. Tholian was furious, because the rest of the earls said it was against the law to hang me for another year. But they hanged poor Konian, and the ship's captain, and all the crew they could catch, and they made me watch. It was just like our luck to land when all the earls had got together to invest that brute Tholian! His grandfather died the week before."

They were now high enough above Neathdale to have, at that moment, an excellent view of the same Tholian's mansion. Moril looked down at its long white front, peaceful and pompous and bowered among trees, and felt like a mouse running over the paws of a cat. He wished the cart was not so very pink and noticeable.

"I'm beginning to think," Kialan said miserably, "that I bring bad luck on people. First Konian, then your father, now Dagner—and goodness knows what happened to the people who helped me escape from Hadd!"

"If you don't mind my asking," Brid said cautiously, "who are you exactly?"

"My father's the Earl of Hannart," said Kialan. "And if you want to dump me out and drive off, I won't blame you."

Moril looked round for Tholian's mansion again. To his relief, it was now hidden by a bend in the road. He was glad. He felt as if this piece of news had put them suddenly in great danger. He was limp with terror, although he knew that they must have been in exactly the same danger from the moment Kialan joined them. Any earl of the South—not only Tholian—would have been overjoyed to get his hands on Kialan. His father was their chief enemy. Anyone found helping Kialan was bound to be savagely punished. Moril thought back, terrified, to Kialan walking through towns so as not to seem to belong to them, sharing the cart in full view of travellers on the road, and even being introduced to Ganner as one of them. And if that was Tholian he had seen in Markind—Moril could hardly bear to think what a risk it had been. Clennen could not have known who Kialan was. He would never have done it for the son of someone he had quarrelled with. But it looked as if Lenina had known.

"I should have known you were from the North," Brid said ruefully, "when you said your name was spelt with a K. They don't use K's in the South, do they? I wondered why Mother told Ganner your name was Collen."

Kialan chuckled slightly. "Your mother's a cool one, isn't she?"

"I suppose she is. But look here—" said Brid. "What were you and your brother doing in the South? Didn't you know what would happen?"

"It was an accident," said Kialan. "Do you remember that storm at the end of April?"

"Yes. We nearly lost the big tent. Remember, Moril?" asked Brid. Moril nodded.

"Well, we nearly got drowned," said Kialan. "We'd been to our aunt on Tulfer Island, and the storm hit us on the way home. We were blown all over the place, and the boat was sitting half under water with sea pouring in, and I don't think the captain knew where we were any more than I did. He said we'd have to get to the nearest haven before we sank. And we did. And it turned out to be Holand. And there were all the earls of the South, smacking their lips at us. To tell you the truth," Kialan said, "I didn't even feel frightened at first. I was so glad to be on land again."

"We were near Holand then," said Brid. "But we never heard—oh yes, Father gave it out as news, didn't he? Is that how Father came into it?"

"Don't you think he was bound to be in on it?" asked Kialan. "He didn't tell me much, but I'm sure he arranged it all. I know the people who helped me escape seemed to spend all the time waiting for messages from the Porter to know what to do next."

"What? Father?" Moril said, puzzled.

"Yes. Your father," said Kialan. "You don't mean to tell me you didn't know he was the Porter?"

"He was *not*!" Brid said angrily. "The Porter's a spy with a price on his head."

"Yes, of course, in the South," said Kialan. "They were mad to catch him here, because he was the main agent for the North. You must have known! He brought all the important messages and

110

most of the refugees. They must have come in this cart. And he organized people here against the earls—I know that, because Konian told me. Konian sent a message to your father for help, during the trial, but it didn't get to him quick enough."

There was a sombre pause. Olob clopped patiently upwards, zig-zagging with the road across the steep hillside, while Brid and Moril tried to take in what Kialan had said. "I thought," Moril said, "that your father had quarrelled with ours?"

"So did I," said Kialan. "But I think that was a pretence. I found out last year—I wish people told me things!—because my father vanished and I needed him for something. And Konian told me to shut up, because he'd gone to meet Clennen the Singer like he always did, but no one was supposed to know. I think they arranged what to do next then."

"I refuse to believe that my Father was a common spy!" said Brid. "Why didn't he *tell* me? He ought to have told me! It's so sneaky, somehow!"

"Don't *shout*!" Moril said, with an anxious look round at Tholian's mansion, which had come into view again, lower down and further off.

Kialan laughed outright. "But he wasn't sneaky! That was the splendid thing about him! I couldn't believe he really was the Porter at first. I saw this fat man with a great big voice, who spent all his time trying to impress people, and I thought there'd been an awful mistake. Then I saw him go into towns, in this shocking bright cart, in a scarlet suit just to make sure people didn't miss him, and sing his head off, and call out at the top of his voice that

111

the price on the Porter's head was two thousand in gold. It was incredible! Then he and your mother would call out messages and hand out notes, right in front of everyone, and I knew half of them were illegal. But no one would believe it, because it was all done so openly. Nobody thought he was anything more than a very good singer. And I really think Clennen thought that was the best joke about it."

Moril blinked a little at this view of his father. But Kialan had hit Clennen off in a way. Clennen *had* treated their shows as a rather serious joke. If he was really the Porter all along, then that would be why. "I suppose that's where Dagner went wrong," he said sadly. "Trying to be secret."

"Dagner was awfully stupid to think he could carry on where Father left off, anyway," said Brid.

"He didn't," said Kialan. "Dagner wasn't trying to do that for a moment. But Clennen asked him to finish off the important things, if he could. Then he was to go North and stay there. And the message to Neathdale was important, because it was about a spy who'd got in among them there."

Moril sighed. He did not say that Dagner thought he had given the message to that very spy. There seemed no point. He said, "Dagner said I was to tell you Henda has asked for a ransom for you. And Tholian is gathering an army."

"Oh damn!" Kialan said wearily. "Then I'll *have* to get through somehow, won't I? You saw Dagner? Tell me."

Moril told Kialan all that happened to him in the jail. He could not help speaking low and looking nervously down at Tholian's mansion each time it came into view. He was relieved when they crossed the brow of the first hill and could not see it any more.

"You were lucky, Moril," said Brid. "If you'd known all the things Kialan's just told us, we might be in jail at this moment." Moril nodded soberly. He certainly could not have acted the surprise he felt when they told him what Dagner had been arrested for. But he knew it had been the merest good luck that he had not happened to mention Kialan.

"I couldn't think," said Kialan, "why Clennen made such a point of not telling you two anything. He wouldn't let me say who I was and neither would Dagner. But I think it saved our skins. I wish it could have saved Dagner's."

"You don't think Dagner was really arrested because of you?" Moril asked.

"I did at first," said Kialan. "I thought we'd all had it, all the time I was sitting in the hedge. I could hardly believe it when I saw the cart coming. No. I think Dagner's trouble is separate, and thanks to you, Moril, they think he just did a bit of freedom-fighting on the side. But I hope it doesn't get round to the Earl. Tholian will put two and two together all right."

"Why did Tholian kill Father?" said Moril.

"He was looking for me," said Kialan, "and he didn't want anyone to know, because I'm supposed to be Hadd's prisoner—or Henda's, only they were still arguing about that when I escaped. Dagner thought that maybe the Neathdale spy—or perhaps it was the fellow they hanged—might have given Tholian a hint about your father. But he couldn't have known much, or we'd all have been arrested. Tholian's the sort who says dead men tell no tales, so he kills Clennen and then beats the woods for me."

"If only we'd known!" said Brid. "Where were you all that time?"

"Up a tree," said Kialan, "rabbits and all. They were crashing about searching all the time you were playing that cwidder, Moril, and it worried them like anything. They kept saying that blessed boy and his music made their heads go round. Tholian suggested going back and killing you too, but none of them could quite be bothered to. And when you left off they'd had enough and they went."

"Could you pass it to me?" said Moril. Kialan obligingly crawled back to the instrument-rack and reached the big cwidder over to the driving-seat. Moril took it and clutched it to him. It felt fat and hard and comforting. Apart from the fact that it seemed to have saved both his life and Kialan's, it was in its rather more awesome way as good as Olob's nose. He felt he needed it, somehow, after the events of today.

"Play something," suggested Kialan.

"No, don't," said Brid. "Not until we've decided what to do. We're slap bang in the middle of Tholian's earldom, and we've obviously got to get North, and everyone knows this cart. And we've no money. I daresay Father meant to go this way because it would have looked suspicious if he didn't, but I vote we turn east and try to get North through the Marshes."

Kialan fetched the map out and scowled at its sketchiness. "I suppose we could try the sea," said Moril. "We might find a boat that wants a singer."

Kialan glared at the map. "We'd take ages, either way. And we can't be more than four days off Flennpass here. Don't either of you understand? Tholian's getting an army together to invade the North, and Henda's sent to my father to say he'll ransom me, so my father thinks I'm a prisoner and daren't do a thing! And I suppose," he added, "Henda's message is the first news my father gets that we're not both drowned. If you don't mind, I'd like to get North as quickly as I can—but it's your cart of course."

Moril glanced at Kialan and decided that his hectoring tone had much to do with the tears in his eyes. Brid did not notice. "Oh, *is* it our cart?" she said. The result was that Kialan managed to laugh, rather sheepishly.

"We'll go straight on," Moril said, suddenly deciding. "We'll do it Father's way and be quite open about it. It worked for him, and it worked for me in the jail."

Brid and Kialan seemed to be relieved that Moril had taken the lead. But, as Olob dragged the cart into the level ground of the first Upland, they began to make nervous objections.

"Innocent little children is all very well," said Brid. "What about when the Earl hears of Dagner doing the Porter's business?"

Moril looked round on fields with green corn showing and sheep grazing. The hills of the North towered against the sky, so high and blue-grey with distance that, on first glance, Moril took them for a bank of cloud.

"A certain pink cart will be looked for," said Kialan. "Could you paint it?"

"Dark green would be best," said Brid. "But we've no money."

A village came in sight, looking very small against the hills of the North. Moril roused himself before Kialan and Brid could have any wilder ideas. "Tholian knows me," he said. "He recognised me up a ladder in Markind. That's the trouble with having red hair."

"Wear a hat," said Kialan.

Moril turned round to quell Kialan. "What about this village?" As he said it, he realised that Kialan was tired out. His face was as white as such a brown complexion could be, and there were dark rings under his eyes. All the watching at night and the suspense in Neathdale had been rather too much for him. "Get down in the cart," Moril said, taking pity on him. "I'll put the cover half up."

Kialan lay thankfully down beside the winejar and Moril pulled the canvas forward until it hid him. They drove straight through the village, Brid holding the reins and Moril sitting beside her, gently strumming the cwidder. On the heights above the village there was an odd little grey tower, belonging to the Lord of the Uplands. Brid looked at it and quivered with terror, knowing as she did that the Earl of Hannart's son was hidden in the cart. But Moril knew it was no different from any other risk they had run without knowing. The tower and the mountains made him think of his imaginary Hannart. He felt soothed and peaceful.

Several people looked up, or out at doors, hearing the cart and the cwidder. When they saw what it was, they smiled and waved. Brid did her best to smile and nod back. Then a woman came out of a house and walked beside them.

"Have you been through Neathdale today?"

"Yes," said Moril.

"They tell me there was to have been a man hanged."

"Yes," said Moril. "He was. We saw him."

"I knew it!" the woman said, smiling. "He was bound to come to it!" She seemed so gleeful that Moril thought she must have hated the hanged man, until he noticed the tears in her eyes. Then he saw she was just trying to hide her feelings. He wanted to say something kind to her, but she left the cart and went back into her house. Moril wondered whether Clennen had known her, and what her connection was with the hanged man.

Chapter IX

A mile or so beyond the village, Olob looked at the sun moving into the blue mountains and turned towards a cart-track which led away to the left. Brid tried to stop him. "No, Olob. We must get on."

"Let him find a place," said Moril. "I told you. It's no good looking guilty. Besides, we haven't eaten a thing since this morning."

"You had a pie, you lucky pig!" snapped Brid, but she gave in and let Olob pull the cart into a secluded grassy space under a cliff. A stream ran in a trickle of green mosses down the rock-face. Moril came down from the cart, feeling shaky at the knees.

"If we're going to camp this near the village," said Kialan, emerging from hiding, "then we'd better set a watch tonight."

"What for?" said Moril. "Nobody's going to bother to come at night, not after three children. And if they come while we're awake, we'll hear them."

"I'm going to watch, all the same," said Kialan.

"No you're not," said Moril. "There's no point."

"Bossy, aren't you, all of a sudden!" Brid snapped. Then she rounded on Kialan. "And if you make yourself ill staying awake every night, what are we supposed to do with you?"

Moril realised that Brid was angry because she was tired and miserable. So he said nothing, and simply began to get Olob out of the shafts. Kialan must have realised it too, because he said wearily, "Oh, all right. I give in," and started collecting firewood.

Brid investigated the provisions Dagner had bought. "What am I supposed to do with all this flour?" she demanded. "And no eggs!"

It looked as if Dagner's idea had been to stock the cart with enough food to last them until they reached the North. But, as Brid said mournfully, his mind must have been on that message, for the only useful things he had bought were the bacon and a large cheese. Among the less useful things were lentils, candles, and a big bunch of rhubarb.

"Look at this!" said Brid, wagging the rhubarb about. "What was he *thinking* of?"

"Waste of money," agreed Kialan. "Did he use all you earned?"

"Yes," said Brid. "Every penny. And there's not even any bread."

They had a rather strange supper of fried bacon, cheese, and experimental pancakes made out of flour and water. Brid, after nibbling one, promptly put them in the frying-pan that held the bacon, and Kialan thought of melting cheese over them to improve the taste. This left them still so empty that they finished the meal with about a quart each of stewed rhubarb —luckily, Lenina had left some sugar in the cart.

Moril felt better after it. He got up, fetched the bucket, and carefully cleaned the cart. It was looking very dusty and uncared for and, to his mind, it had a furtive, illegal look. He thought about Dagner as he worked. He wondered what he had to eat in prison, and how soon he would be tried and hanged. Or did the questioning by the Justice count as a trial? Moril feared that it did. He wondered again what Dagner had said when they questioned him. Then he thought of Dagner trying to carry on Clennen's work in Dagner's way. It had not seemed wise. Dagner had been nervous and secretive and he had made a fatal mistake. But, on the other hand, Dagner was so unlike Clennen that it was probably the only thing he could do. Moril thought about himself going back to Clennen's way, and wondered if that was wise. He was not like Clennen either. But he did not know what he was like. He supposed that, sooner or later, he would have to find out, and then do things in the way best suited to what he found.

Brid and Kialan were washing the pans. Kialan was looking exhausted. Tears kept coming into Brid's eyes, and she angrily wiped them away with the back of her greasy hand. And they were both pretending they were cheerful.

"Do you think if we mixed the cheese in with the flour they'd taste better?" Brid said.

"What about rhubarb? Sort of fritters?" said Kialan.

"Ugh!" said Brid. "When I see Dagner, I'll—" She wiped off another set of tears and said brightly, "He must have had his reasons, I suppose."

Moril tipped away the dirty water, wondering if there could be three more unhappy people in Dalemark. Kialan must know he was a danger to himself and his companions. His landfall in Holand must have been horrible. And since then, Moril realised, Kialan's life had been one long, tense escape, which was not over yet. As for himself and Brid, they had seen their family simply dwindle away, until it was down to their two selves. And Kialan had been fond of Dagner too—fonder than he had realised.

Moril stopped himself in the midst of a snuffle of self-pity. No. Last year, as soon as they were safely in the North, Clennen had told them some of the other things that happened in the South. Whole families had been arrested. The older ones had been hanged, and children younger than Moril had been left with nothing in the world, and nobody dared help them for fear of being arrested too. Clennen had told them how Henda had calmly doubled his taxes last year and turned those who could not pay out to starve; and how old Tholian had hunted an old man with dogs for not raising his hat to him fast enough. Moril knew there must be hundreds of people in the South even worse off than he was. They had a horse and a cart, and Clennen had left them with a means of earning a living and a licence to do it. If it came to the worst, they could go back to Markind. Moril did not like this idea. He tried to tell himself that they could not go back, because of Kialan. But he knew that was not it. Lenina would help Kialan. The reason for his not liking it, he was forced to admit, was because he was not at all clear whether they had deserted Lenina, or she them. And it made him uncomfortable.

"We'll give more shows," he said, putting Lenina out of his mind. He went to the cart to polish the instruments, and stopped at the sight of the winejar taking up so much room inside. "Do you know anything about this winejar?" he called to Kialan.

"No—oh, you mean the papers?" Kialan said, coming over to the cart. "Dagner had a look in Markind, because he had to find the message for Neathdale. They're down inside its basket."

Moril scrambled up to look. Kialan took down the tailgate and told him where to put his hand down between bottle and basket. Brid hurried over and watched Moril fish about, feel paper and pull it out. "What are these?"

"Messages that weren't so important," said Kialan. "Lucky they didn't search the cart, wasn't it?"

Brid and Moril held the papers into the sinking sun and spelt out, in Clennen's writing: *For Mattrick. Someone in Neathdale—I think Halain—smells of lavender. Dirty washing through Pali and Fander in future.*

"Lavender!" said Brid. "Really, Father!"

The other notes said the same, and were marked to be delivered to places between Markind and Neathdale.

"Go and put those all on the fire," Moril said, handing them to Kialan. "Now do you believe we can read?"

Kialan grinned and took the papers. While he was stuffing them under the embers and the air was filling with the strong smell of burning paper, Moril busily worked his hand on round the winejar. Halfway round, he felt more papers. He pulled them out and unfolded them.

These were all in different people's writing. Some of them seemed to have come from parts of the South they had not visited in years. Others concerned the places they had passed through, and these were mostly in Lenina's writing. Moril felt oddly glad to see his mother's small, bold writing. He could see that whatever Lenina had thought, privately, of Clennen's freedom-fighting, she had most scrupulously done what Clennen wanted while he was alive—even at the risk of being hanged for spying. It was queer to find her so honourable, but Moril liked it. Among other things, she had written: *Crady—*169 *taken north to Neathdale and Fledden—*24 *pressed yesterday, with horses.* The other notes said much the same.

"What do you think this means?" said Brid.

Kialan came over to look. "Do you think," he said, after some puzzling, "those might be for my father, or someone in the North? It could be about the army Tholian's gathering."

"You know, I do believe that's it!" said Brid. "They mean how many men went for soldiers from each place. Don't you agree, Moril?"

"Probably," said Moril. It seemed a bit boring to him. "We'd better take them North then." He put them back and, just to be on the safe side, went on working his hand round the other side of the jar. There were cold hard things. He gripped one and pulled it out. "I say!" It was a gold piece. "Whose is this?"

They were all mystified. Brid suggested that it was payment for taking Kialan North, but, as Moril and Kialan rather scornfully pointed out, if Clennen had organized that, he would have been paying himself. No other explanation seemed likely, either.

"Anyway, that means we can buy food tomorrow, Brid said. "Father couldn't mind that."

"Don't be a big idiot!" said Moril. "When did we ever have a gold piece before? Someone's going to think we stole it, and if *we* get arrested the whole thing's going to come out." Carefully, he slipped the coin back behind the basket again.

Brid sighed. "A whole bottleful of gold! Oh, all right. I suppose you're right and it would look odd. I'm going to bed. Get out of the cart."

Moril helped Kialan put up the tent. By then Kialan was so tired that he dragged a blanket into it and fell asleep before the sun set. Moril felt too agitated to go to sleep straight away. He sat against the cliff, with Olob companionably cropping grass nearby, and strummed on the cwidder for comfort. He did not play any particular song, just snatches of this and a bar or so of that. It seemed to express the state of his feelings. He still found it hard to believe that his father had been a notorious agent. Of all the discoveries of the last few days, that one was hardest to take. He had thought he knew Clennen. Now he saw he had not. He wondered when Dagner had found out, and how he had felt. And he made an effort to think of Clennen in this new light.

But, somehow, he did not want to think of his father. He wanted to forget the blood gushing into the lake, and he did not want to consider how Clennen could be so public and so private at one and the same time. Instead, by degrees, Moril took refuge in hazy memories from much earlier. He thought of the cart rolling down a green road in the North. Clennen was singing in the driving-seat, Lenina doing some mending beside him, and the three children playing happily on the lockers. The sun shone—and, somewhat to his surprise, the cwidder began to produce a muzzy sound. It was a very queer noise. Moril did not like it, and Olob looked round at it disapprovingly.

"Time for bed," Moril said to Olob. He got up and went to put the cwidder back in the cart.

Inside the cart was hot, and Brid and the winejar seemed to fill it. Moril hesitated, thinking of the active elbows and knees of Kialan. But he could not bear the heat, so he took a blanket and wriggled into the tent with Kialan.

Luckily, Kialan was so exhausted that he did not move in his sleep. Both he and Moril woke feeling fresher and happier. Brid was the sombre one, but she improved after a breakfast of bacon steaks fried by Kialan. Then Moril fetched Olob's harness to clean. He was determined that their turnout should be as spruce and innocent as he could get it. Kialan, without being asked, went to groom Olob. And Moril realised that, not only had Kialan done his full share of the chores ever since they left Markind, but that nobody had either noticed or thanked him.

"You don't need to do Olob," he said. "I'll do him."

"Am I supposed to stand around and watch you wear yourself out, or something?" said Kialan. "Move, Olob, you lazy lump."

"Well, you used to," said Brid, scrubbing the frying-pan. "And you're an earl's son."

"I thought I'd get that sooner or later!" Kialan said with his most fed-up look. "I didn't know what needed doing at first, and there always seemed loads of you to do it anyway. But if you two are having to earn the money now, it's only fair you don't do everything else."

"Moril," said Brid, going very sombre again, "do you think we really *can* earn money? I mean, even with Dagner, we sounded so—so thin and pale, didn't we?"

"No you didn't," said Kialan, at work on the further side of Olob. "You just gave a different kind of show. Only I think you made a mistake in not building it round Dagner more. You should have got him to sing again, Brid. He'd have done it in short bursts, and his songs are really good."

"They are, aren't they?" Brid said sadly. "And now—"

"Moril," said Kialan, appearing under Olob's nose, "you can't happen to remember Dagner's songs, can you? Enough to play them yourself?"

"I never thought of that!" said Moril. As soon as he had finished the harness, he fetched out the instruments. While Brid set to work polishing them, Moril took up the big cwidder and tried out the first song of Dagner's that came into his head. For some reason, it was the song Dagner had never finished, the one Clennen had forbidden him to sing until they were in the North. Moril stopped after the first few notes, to make sure nobody was about. There seemed to be no one, so he went on. He found he wanted to finish it for Dagner. It seemed the only thing he could do for him.

Dagner had only sketched out part of the tune. Since Moril had no idea what Dagner intended, he let the words take him, this way and that, through a melting blackbird phrase

Come to me, come with me.
The blackbird asks you, "Follow me."

and then to a kind of birdsong triumph in

Wherever you go, I will go.

Kialan seemed almost awestruck. But Brid, as
soon as she realised what song it was, looked up the
cliff and down the slope to make sure they were not
overheard. Moril knew he was breaking the law.
But he wanted to finish the song, so he went, rather
defiantly, on to *The sun is up*. The cwidder produced
a shrill and defiant sound. Moril, cross with himself
for being scared, tried to recapture the first melting
tone and only succeeded in making a scratchy, bad-
tempered tinkle. Dagner would have hated it.
Moril thought of Dagner and put in the first four
lines again at the end, as Dagner had suggested he
might. But he was not thinking very clearly of
Dagner himself—more of Dagner as part of that
happy family on a green road in the North, that
he had pictured the night before. And, just as he
had last night, he heard the cwidder making that
odd, muzzy noise.

Moril sprang up and sprang back. He could not
help it. The cwidder fell on the turf with a melodious thump.

"Moril!" said Brid. "You'll break it!"

"It was splendid!" said Kialan. "Don't stop."

"I don't care!" Moril said hysterically. "I've a
good mind to jump on it! The blessed thing was
playing my *thoughts*! It played the way I was
thinking!"

Brid and Kialan looked at one another, then at
Moril. "Don't you think," Kialan said, "that that's
the way it works? It's your thoughts that bring
out the power."

"But it never did that for Father!" said Moril. "He told me! He said it only did it once."

"Well," Kialan said, rather awkwardly, "he couldn't really use it, could he? It wasn't his kind of thing."

"Except just that one time," said Brid. "Which proves it, Moril. Because it must have been when Father saw Mother in Ganner's hall. And he wanted her to love him instead of Ganner so much that he managed to make the cwidder work, and she did love him enough to come away with him."

After that Moril went and put the cwidder away. Brid got it out again and polished it for him, but he pretended not to notice. When Olob, the cart and all the instruments were gleaming with care, they set off again through the first Upland, towards the steep hill to the second. Brid drove. Moril sat beside her, trying out another of Dagner's songs on his small treble cwidder. But it was no good. The treble cwidder just felt foolish and flimsy and shrill, and it sounded terribly ordinary. As Olob settled into a slow, heaving walk up the steep hill into the next Upland, Moril was forced to turn and ask Kialan to put the little cwidder away and pass him the big one.

The matter-of-fact way Kialan handed it to him made Moril feel much better about it. Moril took the cwidder thankfully. It felt right. He was not sure now whether it was a comfort or a burden, but if Kialan could accept so easily that it was a powerful and mysterious thing, so could he. But he knew he was going to have to learn to control the thing. You could not earn your living with a cwidder that whined if you were miserable and croaked if you were cross. "How should I start?" he asked Kialan over his shoulder.

Kialan hesitated, not because he did not understand Moril, but because he was not sure how Moril should start. "Understanding yourself perhaps?" he asked. "I mean, I've no idea either, but try that. Er—why didn't you stay in Markind, for instance? Was it just seeing Tholian there?"

Moril, by this time, was sure that it was not. "Why didn't *you* want to stay?" he asked Brid, as a start. "Duty to Father?"

"Like Mother, you mean?" said Brid. "N—no. A bit of that. I do prefer Father's outlook to Mother's —but it was really almost more like the way Mother went back to Ganner. It's what I'm used to—this— and nothing else felt right."

Moril felt that went for him too. But there was more to it than that. He could have persuaded Brid to go back to Markind after Dagner was arrested, but he had not thought of it even. He had not wanted to go back when he had found out how dangerous their journey North really was. And he was still going North, as if it was a matter of course. Why?

"Why, Moril?" asked Brid.

"I was born in the North," Moril answered, rather slowly. "When I—er—dream of things, it's always the North. And the North is right and the South is wrong."

"Bravo!" said Kialan.

Moril turned to smile at him. He found himself turning from the towering unseeable hills of the North to a low, blue vision of the South, beyond Kialan's head. "But I still don't understand," he said.

At the top of the hill there was a village, a very small place, simply ten houses and an alehouse, clinging to the steep brow of the hill.

"Don't let's perform here," said Brid. "There's a bigger place further on, I know."

They went past the village into a wider Upland, full of grazing sheep. By the middle of the morning, Moril's cwidder was sounding melancholy. "I can't see us getting much," he said. "Not just the two of us."

"Would it help at all," said Kialan, "if I were to pretend to be Dagner?"

Both their heads whipped round his way. It was almost a marvellous idea.

"Would they remember Dagner from last year?" said Kialan.

"We didn't perform in the Uplands at all last year," said Brid. "But—"

"I've been thinking," said Kialan. "No one but the earls knows I'm in the South. And it's so out of the way here that no one's going to know Dagner was arrested unless we tell them. I think it would be safe enough—and a bit in your father's style, too."

Moril made the obvious objection. "You can't sing." They looked at one another for a moment. Moril remembered Kialan listening in to his lessons with Clennen, appearing in the crowd whenever they gave a show, and seeming so knowledgeable the time the big cwidder went out of tune. "Or can you?" said Moril.

"Not as well as you," said Kialan, "but—may I borrow one of these cwidders for a moment?"

"Go ahead," said Brid.

Kialan took up Dagner's cwidder and tuned it without needing to be given a note. Moril and Brid looked at one another. Neither of them could do that. And from the moment Kialan started to play, they knew they were listening to a gifted person very much out of practice. If he did not sing as well as he played, it was merely because he was the age when his voice still moved troublesomely from low to high. Moril vividly remembered the trouble Dagner had had at the same age.

What Kialan sang was a song of the Adon's, one that Clennen never sang in the South.

> *Unbounded truth is not a thing*
> *Cramped to time and bound in place—*

"Ooh!" said Brid, looking nervously round.

"No one about. Shut up!" said Moril.

Kialan did that part meticulously in the right old style. But then he gave Moril a bit of a wink and dropped into the same kind of different fingering Moril had used in Neathdale. The song seemed to come alive.

> *Truth strangely changes space,*
> *By right of its reality.*
> *It moves the hills containing me*
> *Wider than the world, or small*
> *As in a nut. Truth is free*
> *And laws are stones, or not at all,*
> *And men without it nothing.*

"Oh, I liked that!" said Moril.

"I took a leaf out of your book," Kialan said, rather apologetically. "I don't like the old style either, and I don't see why old things should be sacred. Wow! I'm out of practice, though! Do you think I'll be any use to you?"

"You know you will," said Brid. "You big fraud. If you're that good, why on earth didn't you say so before? Father would have put you in the show, instead of making you walk through all the towns."

"I know he would!" Kialan said feelingly. "He'd have dressed me in scarlet and flaunted me. I didn't quite like to say anything at first—you were all so excellent—and as soon as I realised what your father was like, I'd have died rather than tell him. It was frightening enough walking."

The upshot of this was that Olob quietly pulled the gleaming cart on to the green of the village a mile or so on, and three people stood up to sing and play. Moril and Kialan were nervous, Brid, as usual, as confident as a queen. Moril did one or two of Dagner's songs, but mostly they sang ballads, since those were Brid's speciality and Kialan's voice was not equal to anything more difficult. A scattering of people listened and clapped. Someone asked for an encore, and Brid gave them *Cow-Calling*. They got a little money, enough to buy eggs, milk and butter, and a woman gave Brid a basket of somewhat withered apples. It was not a raving success, but it was no failure either.

"We can do it!" said Brid.

Moril smiled, and strummed his cwidder as they took to the road again. Every so often, he played a tune in earnest, and Kialan would come in too on Dagner's cwidder. Kialan was getting more in practice every moment. They experimented, and tried for effects and new settings. Moril had seldom enjoyed making music so much. He almost wished the distance to Hannart were twice as long.

Chapter X

They had a sort of cheese omelette for lunch, sitting on a point of green land between two brisk streams. Kialan would have it that what they were eating was scrambled eggs. Brid disagreed. Moril did not join in the argument because he was listening to the sound of the water. It made him think of the North. The sound of water running was never far away in the North. He was dreamily considering whether one could make a tune that captured the noise, when Brid shook him sharply and told him they were moving.

"You didn't have to do that!" said Kialan.

"Why not? *You* know how maddening he is when he goes into a dream," Brid retorted.

"Yes, but it's just his way," said Kialan. "He's about six times as awake as most people really. I bet he heard every word we said—didn't you, Moril?"

"I suppose I did," Moril said, in some surprise.

"Can I drive this next stretch?" Kialan asked.

Neither Brid nor Moril objected. Letting Kialan drive Olob seemed the best way to show he was a full member of the company now, and not a passenger any longer. So Kialan held the reins, and Olob clopped onward through the lonely Upland. Moril sat beside him, still strumming the cwidder, looking dreamily round at the hills, the flocks of sheep and the occasional shepherd in the distance.

They came to a steep rise to the third and last Upland. It was the highest and also the most beautiful of the three climbs, because it was clothed in trees the whole way up. The road, though it was the main road, dwindled to a rutty lane, damp and stony, boring its way upwards through the woods. The sunlight fell in gay splashes through the bright leaves of springtime. All three of them looked upward and grinned at the way their faces became speckled and greenish.

But Olob, whether he objected to Kialan holding the reins or to having to climb two steep hills in one day, became steadily more restive. At first it was simply tossing his head and stopping. Kialan persuaded him to move again, each time with more difficulty. But, as they went on upwards, Olob took to trampling this way and that, so that the cartwheels caught in the hawthorns at the side of the road. Kialan grew exasperated. The fourth time Olob did it, Kialan lost his temper and swore at Olob. Olob promptly turned right across the road and seemed to be trying to climb the sheer bank into the woods. Moril thought the cart would overturn. The winejar fell over and knocked Brid sideways, with a dreadful twanging of cwidders.

"Let me take him," said Moril.

Kialan crossly handed him the reins. Moril propped the cwidder across his knees and worked with both hands and some shouting to persuade Olob back on to the road again. Olob refused to come out of the bushes.

"What's got into him?" said Kialan.

"No idea," said Moril. As he said it, two memories came to him. One was of almost exactly the same conversation, between himself and Lenina, just before Tholian came out of the wood and killed Clennen. The other was of Olob behaving like a colt in Neathdale, just before Dagner was arrested. "Quick!" he said to Kialan. "There are enemies near and Olob knows. Get out and go through the woods until we've passed them."

"How *can* he know?" said Kialan, with his most fed-up look.

"I don't know, but he does. Father always said he wouldn't part with Olob for an earldom, and I think that's why. Get *out*, I said!" Moril said urgently.

"Do as you're told, Kialan!" said Brid from the tilted bottom of the cart.

Kialan, entirely unconvinced, swung himself grudgingly down from the cart. As Olob was halfway through a bush, up the right bank of the road, Kialan went up beside him by the space he had cleared, and vanished among the trees higher up. Moril could hear his cross footsteps swishing along the steep hillside.

"Go quietly!" he said, but he could tell Kialan took no notice. Moril dumped the cwidder in the canted cart and went to Olob's head. Olob was most unwilling to leave the bush. "I know, old fellow, but we've got to go on and look innocent," Moril said. "*Come* on, now!"

It took some time to get Olob back on the road. When he did consent to come, Brid had to lean on the cart to keep it upright. Then she climbed in and tried to set the winejar and the instruments to rights. Olob reluctantly climbed onwards. Above them in the woods, Kialan's feet kept pace with the cart, swishing loudly and cracking twigs. Moril wished he would not make so much noise.

Olob toiled round three corners and Brid still seemed to be busy in the cart. "What are you doing?" Moril asked.

"Putting my boots on," said Brid. "If there *are* enemies near, I'm going to look respectable. And I'm putting the sharp knife down the right boot." She joined him shortly, looking flushed and determined, firmly booted. "I'll drive," she said.

Moril gave her the reins, and hung the cwidder round his neck by its strap, which, he supposed, was his way of looking respectable. His boots, by this time, were nothing like as new and smart as Brid's. Brid was better at managing Olob. Olob put on a great act of this being the most difficult climb of his life and did everything in his power to suggest that they turned back, but Brid kept him going. Beyond the protesting clatter of his hoofs, Moril listened for Kialan, but he could not hear him any longer. By this time, they were near the top of the climb. They rounded what must have been the last corner, and Olob shied.

"Clever Olob," Brid remarked.

There was a stout wooden trestle in the road. It did not fill the road, but it was placed so that there was no room for a cart to pass on either side. There were a number of men with it, one of them sitting on the trestle. To Moril's dismay, they were all in full war-gear. Each of them wore a steel cap and a steel breastplate with a pointed front—which gave them all chests like pigeons—over jackets and trousers of tough leather. They wore great black boots and long swords in black leather scabbards.

Brid drew the alarmed Olob up. "Would you mind moving that trestle? We need to get by," she said haughtily. She was frightened and daunted, but there were enough soldiers to make her feel as if she had an audience.

Three of the men strolled forward. None of them made any effort to move the trestle. "What's your business?" said one. The other two strolled on and looked over the sides of the cart to see what was in it.

"Drunkards, by the look of this wine," one said, and both of them sniggered a little.

"We're singers," said Brid. "Can't you see?"

"In that case, let's see your licence," said the first man, and held out his hand for it. Brid, after a moment's hesitation, fetched the licence out of the locker under the seat and handed it to him. He looked at it casually. "Which of you is Clennen?"

"That's my father," said Brid. "He was killed four days ago."

"Then you haven't got a licence," said the man. "Have you?"

"Yes we have," said Brid. "We're entitled to sing under that licence for six months. That's the law, and you can't tell me it isn't."

"That may be the law in the other earldoms, but not in the South Dales," the man said, grinning. "You haven't read the small print." He unrolled the parchment and pointed vaguely to the bottom of it. When Brid leant over to look, he took it out of reach and let it roll up again. "Too bad," he said. "You'd better come and explain yourselves."

"It doesn't say that at all!" Brid said furiously. "You're just using it as an excuse. That licence is perfectly in order, and you know it!"

The man stopped grinning. "You'll do as you're told," he said. He nodded to one of the other men, who took hold of Olob's bridle. The rest moved the trestle aside. The one holding Olob hauled on him and Olob, passively resisting for all he was worth, was forced to move reluctantly on. Brid and Moril were towed after him, feeling quite helpless. It was clear that someone—Tholian, probably—had given orders that all travellers were to be stopped. Moril looked back to see the soldiers putting the trestle across the road again and sitting on it to wait for any other comers. He wondered about jumping off the cart and running. But there was a soldier walking on either side of it and it did not seem worth trying. Their only hope seemed to be to use Clennen's method and appear as open and innocent as they knew how.

They went fifty yards or so—a difficult jerky fifty yards, because Olob was extremely frightened and did not want to move, in spite of the names the soldier called him—and came to a steep road branching to the right. The soldier dragged Olob into it. Moril had forgotten this road. It worried him that Kialan would have to cross it on his way to the last Upland.

"Where does this road go?" he asked Brid.

"To a sort of extra valley at one side," Brid said. "We camped there the year before last. Don't you remember? Moril, they will let us go, won't they?"

Moril glanced down at the soldiers. "We haven't done anything wrong," he said carefully. But the winejar came into his mind as he said it, and he wondered why on earth he had not left it behind somewhere.

A twig snapped in the wood up to the right. Moril looked up. And looked away quickly, in case the soldiers noticed. He had a very clear sight of Kialan staring down at the cart, alarmed and rather puzzled, as if he had not gathered what was going on. Moril stared at the steep road ahead and tried to will Kialan to cross the road while he had the chance and go on North. But he was very much afraid Kialan intended to follow the cart.

The trees opened like the end of a tunnel and they came out into the valley. Brid gave a little moan. Beyond two groups of soldiers, evidently on guard, were tents, weapons, horses and many more soldiers, as far as they could see. It was a long, thin valley, and winding, so that half of it was out of sight. But they had no doubt that the part of it they could not see was also full of soldiers and weapons and tents.

The nearest tent was a very large one. There was a chair outside it, and in that chair sat Tholian. His head turned as the cart came out from among the trees. As far as he could tell from this distance, Moril thought Tholian smiled. And he saw that Clennen's method was not going to help them here. In fact, he doubted if any method was going to be much use.

"Get down," one of the soldiers said to Brid and Moril.

They climbed down, Brid a little awkward in her boots, Moril clutching the cwidder, and stood where they had a lower and even busier view of the teeming valley ahead. Moril dimly remembered that the year before last there had been fields and crops growing here. There was no sign of them now. As they were taken towards Tholian, he saw nothing but men drilling and training, all down the valley. It was filled with orders and curses, and the thick warm smell of many people and horses. The grass, and any crops there might have been, was trampled to earth, except for a green stretch round the large tent where Tholian sat.

Tholian signalled to the soldiers to make Brid and Moril stand to one side of the patch of grass, and turned his pale eyes from them to the soldiers. "Just these two in the cart?" he asked.

Moril seized the opportunity to look over his shoulder to see what had become of Olob and the cart. He was glad to find one of the soldiers struggling to tie the unwilling Olob to a tree beside the road.

"Could I have your attention, Cousin?" he heard Tholian say, and he turned back hurriedly. Tholian sounded irritated. But, when Moril looked at him, he was smiling. He could have been friendly in spite of his queer, shallow eyes. "We are related aren't we?" he said.

Moril thought about it. "I suppose so. But it's Mother who's your cousin."

"Once removed," said Tholian. "Which makes us twice removed, I believe."

"I'm surprised you acknowledge it at all," said Brid. "Considering—"

"Why not?" said Tholian. "It doesn't hurt you. But don't deceive yourselves into thinking your mother's going to get a penny of dowry out of me.

I'm content to do as my grandfather wanted. Ganner's a fool if he thinks I'm going to make him rich on Lenina's account."

This seemed a very odd thing for Tholian to start talking about. Moril wondered if he was a trifle mad. "I shouldn't think Ganner does think that," he said.

"He's fond of Mother, you see," explained Brid.

Tholian laughed. "Fool, isn't he?" He was so contemptuous that Brid all but sprang to Ganner's defence. "But I stayed for the wedding," Tholian said, before Brid could speak, "which was more than you did. You threw Ganner into a fine old fuss by leaving like that, you know. Your mother took it much more calmly. So I promised them I'd look out for you on the road and send you back to Markind when I found you."

"That was kind of you," Brid said coldly. Nevertheless, both she and Moril were beginning to feel distinctly easier. If Tholian were regarding them simply as silly young relations and himself as doing Ganner a favour, then the position was nothing like as bad as they had feared. It would be exasperating to be sent back to Markind, but at least Kialan, with luck, could get North on foot from here.

"Didn't Mother recognize you?" Moril said slowly, rather puzzled at the way Tholian was now being a friend of the family.

"Of course," Tholian said, not at all disconcerted. "But, as I'm Ganner's overlord, there wasn't much she could say. Not that she would. She has a way of saying things in silence, your mother. By the way, what became of your brothers?"

They saw he had just been showing them how much he knew. It gave them both a jolt. Moril reacted best, because he was able to rely on his habitual sleepy look. He went on staring at Tholian in a vague, friendly way, though he had never felt less vague or less friendly in his life. But Brid was so shaken that she had to put on an act.

"Funny you should ask," she said, with artificial brightness. "We don't quite know—"

"Yes, we do, Brid," Moril said, fearing she was going to babble herself into trouble. "Dagner went back to Markind." It was a risky thing to say, but Moril knew that if Tholian already knew that Dagner had been arrested and why, it did not matter what he said anyway.

"Did he indeed?" said Tholian, and there was no telling whether he had heard about Dagner or not. "And what about the other brother—er—Collen, was it?"

Moril knew Tholian had not seen Kialan in Markind. If he had, none of them would have been allowed to leave. He must have heard Ganner talk about him later. And no one would be surprised to find Ganner had got something wrong. Moril opened his mouth to say they had not got another brother, but Brid, to his annoyance, came in first, with tremendous verve: "Oh, Collen! He's so stupid you never know *what* he'll do! But we think he went with Dagner."

"Curious," said Tholian. His untrustworthy eyes slid over Brid, and over her again. "Now I thought I was reliably informed that there were three of you giving a show in Updale this morning."

That had obviously been a fatal mistake. But

how could they have known Tholian was so near? The only thing to do was to say that the third one had been Dagner. Moril drew breath to say it, but, once more, Brid rushed in. "Yes, of course. But that's what I was telling you. Collen went back after that. He said he was going to Neathdale and he—er—he got a lift in a farm waggon."

Moril sadly wished that Brid would let him do the talking. Brid was not as clever as she thought she was. No doubt she thought she was doing very well, but she had first admitted Kialan's existence and now that he was quite near, and Moril knew there was no need to have done either. Tholian had never seen Kialan in their company. He was only going by guess. But now he was almost certain. He was looking at Brid, worrying her by just looking, and obviously enjoying the way he was worrying her.

"I don't think you quite understand the position," Tholian said, when Brid, flushed and alarmed, had dropped her eyes from his pale ones to her boots. "I'm ready to send you both back to Markind safely, in exchange for Kialan Kerilsson. Not otherwise. Is that understood now?"

"I don't understand you at all," Brid said valiantly.

Tholian looked at Moril. "Do you?"

Moril tried to repair some of the damage Brid had done by saying, "Not really. Who's this person you're talking about?"

The only result of this was that Tholian turned his eyes back to Brid. "Keril," he said, "as I'm sure you know, is Earl of Hannart." Without bothering to turn round, he snapped his fingers to some of the men near. They came hurrying up. "Listen," said Tholian. "Kialan Kerilsson is about five foot seven, solidly built, with a dark complexion and fair hair. His nose is aquiline and his eyes are much the same colour as mine. Start searching the woods for a boy of that description."

The men at once turned and went hurrying further into the thronged valley. Brid, as Moril knew she would, showed her consternation by saying, with horrible brightness, "What a queer kind of person that sounds!"

"No, no," said Tholian. "Just a typical Northerner." Beyond him, captains waved their arms and shouted orders. In a matter of seconds, quite a surprising number of soldiers left off drilling and moved at a run towards the woods behind Moril and Brid. Moril could only hope that Kialan had had the sense to cross the road and go North as fast as he could. Tholian's eyes moved sideways to make sure his orders were being carried out, and then turned back to Brid. "You seem worried," he said, and laughed at her.

"Not in the least," Brid lied haughtily.

"But you don't," said Tholian, looking at Moril. "Why not?"

Moril did not see why Tholian should make a game of him. "Why did you kill my father?" he said.

Tholian was not in the least discomposed. The cool way he took the question upset Moril more than a little. It reminded him of Lenina. "Now, why was it?" Tholian said, pretending to remember. Moril thought of Lenina coolly stopping Clennen's bleeding and saw an actual family likeness to Lenina in Tholian's calm face. He wished he had not seen it. "I was having a little trouble finding Kialan," said Tholian, "as I recall. But I think the main reason I killed him was that it was probable he was the Porter."

Brid gasped, which amused Tholian. Moril felt hopeless, though he managed not to show it. "If you thought that, why didn't you have him arrested?" he said.

"Legally, instead of murdering him," said Brid, who was in such despair that she no longer cared what she said.

"But that would have been a silly thing to do," Tholian said laughingly. "A man arrested and tried for crimes like the Porter's very easily becomes a hero. You hang him, and people take his side, or even rebel in his memory. Besides, I've seen Clennen give his shows in Neathdale. And I really didn't see why he should be given the chance to put on the biggest performance of his life. He'd have enjoyed it too much."

"You—" Brid hunted for the nastiest word she knew. "Fiend!" she said. Tholian, of course, laughed.

Moril said nothing. Up till then he had disliked Tholian, and he was afraid of him, because he was powerful and had such queer eyes. But after that, he hated him, violently and personally. He should have hated him before, he supposed, but the fact was that, in an odd way, he had thought of Clennen's death almost as if it were an accident, unfair in the way accidents were. Now he knew Tholian had intended it to be unfair, he hated Tholian for it.

"And how did you find Father?" Brid said. "Did Ganner tell you, you murdering beast!"

Tholian, luckily for Brid, still seemed to find her funny. "Ganner? Oh no," he said. "I don't have to rely on Ganner for information. Though I must say, Ganner didn't seem to be breaking his heart over Clennen when I told him he was dead." He laughed. "I suppose we put Ganner in a bit of a spot," he said, "all turning up in Markind almost together that day." He looked at Brid, to see how she took that. Brid realised Tholian was trying to torment her. She stared haughtily away at the busy soldiers in the valley. Tholian's eyes looked past her, at something behind them. "One last thing," he said. "Never try to carry on like your father. It's stupid, and it never pays. If I'd copied my father, I wouldn't be here with an army."

There was a nasty reasonableness about this that annoyed Moril. "Yes, but you see," he said, "it was something that needed doing."

Tholian was not interested any longer. He stood up. "Bring him here," he said. "Move, can't you!"

A group of soldiers hurried up, dragging Kialan. Kialan was dishevelled and red in the face. Twigs were clinging to his clothes. He was resisting rather, but he also had his head bowed in the sullen way Moril had seen among the prisoners in Neathdale. It was the way you looked, Moril realised, when you were caught. You had it whether you were guilty or innocent. It did not surprise him that Kialan was caught. He had made the mistake of staying near the cart. No doubt he had hoped to help Brid and Moril. Perhaps, since he was now the eldest, he had felt responsible for them. But Moril did not feel one twinge of gratitude. He just felt sad. Kialan had hung about, and Brid had made sure Tholian guessed he was near. That was the trouble with people who thought too well of themselves.

Chapter XI

"Ah! Kialan!" said Tholian. "Nice to see you where there aren't any other earls to interfere."

Kialan looked up at Tholian from among the soldiers, with his head still a little bowed, but did not answer. Moril noticed that it was indeed true as Tholian had said, that Kialan's eyes were almost the same colour as Tholian's. It made him see the difference between them. For Kialan, scared and sullen though he was, had a direct and living look, and Tholian's eyes were blank and strange. It was clear that, while Tholian thought of Brid and Moril as rather funny and not at all important, he thought of Kialan as quite another matter.

"I thought you'd appear on this road sooner or later," Tholian said. "But we were watching the Marshes too, in case. I'm hoping to let your father know you really are our prisoner. You'll have to write him a letter."

"I'm blowed if I shall!" said Kialan. "Write it yourself."

"Very well. I will," agreed Tholian. "I suppose he'll recognise one of your ears, if I send it with the letter. Hold him tightly," he said to the soldiers. He took a knife from a sheath at his belt and walked towards Kialan.

Kialan tried to back away and was held in place by two soldiers. "All right," he said hurriedly. "I'll write you a letter if you want." Moril did not blame him.

But Tholian took no notice. The blank look in his eyes did not alter. The soldiers screwed up their faces. Moril, sickened and terrified, realised that Tholian just wanted an excuse to hurt Kialan. He clutched the cwidder and wondered what he could do. Kialan, even more frightened, tried to duck his head away from the knife. "Hold him, I said!" said Tholian.

One of the soldiers took a handful of Kialan's hair. Brid, without really thinking what she was doing, plunged forward and tried to catch hold of Tholian's arm. She got no further than the nearest soldier, who pushed her sharply away. Brid staggered back and bumped into Moril, jolting his right hand on the cwidder, so that he accidentally struck a long humming note from the deepest string.

An extraordinary buzzing numbness filled the air and seemed to be eating up Moril's brain. He could do nothing, and barely think. The noise pressed into his head and forced him down on his knees. Everything outside his head was grey and pulsating, burring and blurred, and the feeling went on and on and on. He thought he saw Tholian, looking a little bewildered, stand still and slowly sheath his knife, while Kialan and the soldiers all shook their heads like people who have been hit. Brid pressed both hands to her eyes. Their movements made Moril feel sick. He knelt with his head bent, looking at the pulsing earth, and wondered if he was going to die.

Brid knelt down beside him. "Moril, are you all right? It was the cwidder, wasn't it?" Moril shook his humming head at her, wanting her to be quiet.

Everyone except Moril seemed to have quite recovered, except that Tholian looked puzzled, as if he had forgotten a word that was on the tip of his tongue. "Tie him up for now," he said to the soldiers, in a rather irritated way. "Get some rope, one of you."

"You made Tholian forget!" Brid whispered. "Do attend, Moril. You might be able to do it again." But Moril could not attend. His face was so white that Brid became worried, which meant that she was very cross with him, in a harsh, snapping whisper which hurt Moril's numbed head. Then Brid suddenly jumped to her feet and dashed away from him. "You can't do that!" she shouted. "It's cruel!"

That jerked Moril to his senses. He looked up and saw Kialan had been tied with his hands behind him to one of the stakes that carried the tent-ropes. The reason for Brid's outcry was that Tholian, not satisfied with merely tying him, had put a noose round Kialan's tied hands and was hoisting them up his back. The effect must have been like having both arms twisted at once. Moril could see Kialan was in agony.

Tholian turned to Brid as soon as he had made the rope fast. "Can't?" he said. "Go back to your brother." When Brid did not move at once, Tholian advanced on her, with his strange eyes blank. "Are you going to do as I said?"

Brid was frightened enough to turn and run back to Moril. As she came, she mouthed, "*Do something!*"

Tholian started off towards where several captains were hovering, wanting to speak to him. "Those two are not to move from there," he said over his shoulder to the soldiers round Kialan.

"Moril," whispered Brid. "The cwidder. Make it undo the rope."

Moril wished he could. He was sure the cwidder was quite capable of releasing Kialan, if only he knew how to work it. Osfameron had made it move mountains. But Moril had not the slightest idea how to begin and was very much afraid of making a mistake and bringing that awful humming into his own brain again. Kialan tried to give him a brave look, although he was grinning with pain. Moril could see him struggling to get into a more comfortable position when there was no way of doing so. And Tholian might leave him like that for hours. It was worth a try.

Remembering the way the cwidder seemed to play his thoughts, Moril set himself to imagine Tholian's noose pulling and twisting Kialan into that unnatural position. It was horrible. His arms ached and sweat dropped out from under his hair. He thought fiercely, this must *stop*! and gently touched the slack bottom string.

It chimed like a soft, deep bell. Moril braced himself against the humming, but it did not come. Its effect, though it was not at all what he expected, was on Kialan alone. He saw Kialan's head suddenly drop and his knees give. He did not move, and it was clear that only the ropes were holding him up. Terrified, Moril clapped his hand across the string and stopped it vibrating.

Brid rounded on Moril with tears whisking down her cheeks. "You stupid idiot! You've killed him!"

"Shut up!" Moril whispered, anxiously watching both Kialan and the soldiers just beyond him. "They'll realise. Look. He's breathing. He's only passed out."

"But what about the ropes?" Brid whispered.

Moril shook his head. "I can't. I was trying to. I think I can only make it work on people."

One of the soldiers turned and saw Kialan sagging. When Tholian came back from talking to the captains, they pointed Kialan out to him. Tholian simply shrugged and passed by on his way somewhere else.

"I *hate* Tholian!" said Brid.

Moril said nothing. He knelt on the ground, nursing his cwidder, thinking as he had never thought in his life before. The soldiers, meanwhile, looked at one another, looked round to see how far away Tholian was, and undid the noose from Kialan's hands, so that Kialan slid to his knees with his head hanging almost upside down.

"Look, Moril," Brid whispered. "You did undo the ropes, sort of."

Moril had seen perfectly well, though he gave no sign of it. He was as alert as he had been in the jail in Neathdale. He could have told Brid exactly how many captains, troops and horsemen there were in the part of the valley they could see. He was aware of every time a group of new recruits came marching in, and how many came in each group. Four groups arrived while he knelt and thought and while Kialan hung in a heap, head downwards. Moril saw that they did not come by the road, but down through the woods, to keep their mustering secret. He also saw that almost every new arrival was miserable. They trailed their feet and held their heads at that sullen angle Kialan and Dagner had both held theirs when they knew they were caught. He could see that few of them had joined Tholian's army willingly. But he was thinking, thinking. For he was sure that the cwidder he was hugging on his knees was capable of saving all three of them and getting them North with news of Tholian's army. He knew how it could be done. The only thing he did not know was how to call up the power in the cwidder to do it.

Since it was his thoughts the cwidder responded to, Moril tried to understand how he might feed his entire self through it into the enormous power he knew was needed. His father had said Moril was in two halves. "Come together," Clennen had said, "and there's no knowing what you might do." Moril supposed Clennen had meant the way Moril was incorrigibly dreamy and also unbelievably alert at times, just as he was now. But, as Kialan had noticed, he was often both at the same time, unless he went vague in self-defence. Moril thought that could not quite be it.

But there was another way he was in two halves. His mother was a Southern aristocrat, and his father a freedom-fighting singer from the North. As Dagner had said, there was no doubt it was a weird mixture. It was cold and hot, strict and free, restrained and outspoken, all at once. The trouble was, this did not quite add up to Moril. He did not think he had inherited much from his Southern ancestry—certainly none of the unfeeling tyranny that made his distant cousin Tholian so detestable.

But Tholian's calm cruelty had, in a horrible way, reminded him of Lenina. Moril remembered Kialan saying "Your mother's a cool one". And that was it, of course. Lenina never lost her head, and neither did Moril. He knew that, if Brid had only let him, he could coolly have led Tholian to believe that none of them had ever set eyes on Kialan, just as Lenina might have done. Keeping your head was part of the strict standard of the South. It was the same strict standard that had kept Lenina so loyal to Clennen, even though she hated life in the cart and disagreed with the freedom-fighting. And Moril saw that it was the same kind of strict loyalty that had brought him north—only, with him, it was loyalty to the North.

After this followed something very uncomfortable, which Moril would not have faced if he had not had such a pressing need to use the cwidder. He had to admit he had deserted Lenina. He had gone off and left her, when she had been trying to make them happy. He hoped he had not made her too unhappy, because he knew that seeing Tholian in Markind had only given him the excuse he had been looking for to go North. And, going off like that, he had been trying to deny the Southern part of him—all the strict, honourable things which were the good aspect of the South. It did not do to deny them, even though he thought he had been doing it out of loyalty to Clennen.

Then he tried to find out what he had got from Clennen. Goodness knew what strange blood the singers came from. They could all sing and play. They saw a little more than most people, and some of them dreamed dreams. But Moril knew that all he had got from Clennen himself were ideas of freedom and his love of the North. The rest was the common stock of the singers.

The puzzling part was that these two halves added up to three quite different people, Brid, Dagner and Moril. Brid had Lenina's sharpness and some of Lenina's efficiency, and she had Clennen's love of an audience, without Clennen's gifts—though she thought she had them. Dagner had far more of the gifts, but he had all Lenina's reserve, and more. In fact, it had been very much in Lenina's manner that Dagner had set off north to finish Clennen's work for him, knowing he had not the personality to do it. None of them had inherited the largeness that made Clennen what he was. And why had Clennen not told Brid or Dagner they were in two halves?

Moril found himself suddenly at a dead end. He saw he would have to get at the cwidder's power some other way. He had to. The third batch of recruits had just arrived. The valley was filling with soldiers, and the North did not know. And the Earl of Hannart would not dare move because of Kialan. And Moril knew Kialan was actively in danger from Tholian. Tholian passed several times, and each time he looked at Kialan's hanging body as if he wanted it awake and writhing.

Moril thought of the cwidder itself. Though Osfameron could use it on things, it seemed that Moril was only going to make it have an effect on people. That was right for music, in a way. You performed, and people listened and were affected by it. So what did you put into a performance to bring out the power?

Moril did not know. He had only the vaguest idea what he had done to make Kialan unconscious. All right, he thought. What *didn't* my father do, that he could never use the power more than once? And he thought of Clennen, from day to day, as he had known him, huge, genial and sociable—and boring Kialan stiff by telling the same story three times over. He thought of the way Clennen had been the Porter, quite openly, enjoying deceiving people by the simple fact that he did it all in public, as obviously as possible. Kialan had been positive that this was what Clennen enjoyed particularly. Then Moril thought of Clennen saying "Remember that" so often—almost as if he hoped one of them might write all his sayings down one day. Perhaps Brid would, Moril thought, smiling a little. Then he remembered a particular saying of Clennen's, the day they picked Kialan up. Clennen had said the cart was like life. "You may wonder what goes on inside, but what matters is the look of it and the kind of performance we give." Later on, Clennen had asked Dagner about another saying, and Dagner had got this one wrong. "Something about life being only a performance," Dagner had said.

And that was it, Moril thought. Clennen was all performance. Layers of performance. He was the best singer in Dalemark and he used it to play the Porter, and he was the Porter because he was using his sincere feelings about freedom to play the singer —to and fro, over and under, Clennen had performed, even to his own family. His whole life had said *Look at me*! He had known he was a performer, and he had used that knowledge, just as Brid had used her real sorrow to perform with in Neathdale.

But he could not use the cwidder. It was not going to say *Look at me*! It did not work like that.

If you did not say *Look at me*!, what was the right way? With a joyous feeling of being on the right track, Moril thought of Dagner next. Kialan had called what was really Dagner's performance, "A different kind of show". Moril felt warmly grateful to Kialan. Kialan pointed things out. If only because of this, Kialan deserved to be rescued and taken back to the warm-hearted, cocksure, outspoken North where he belonged.

But Dagner—Dagner had been diffident. He had never said *Look at me*! because he was shy when people did. What he did was to show people his thoughts—a little—in his songs. "Look here," he seemed to say. "Excuse me. This is what I think. I hope you like it." And people did like it—not in the way they appreciated Clennen, but as if they had been told something new.

Moril knew he was unable—at least for the present—to make something new, just as he was unable to use his real feelings for show, like Brid. That left the old songs, Moril's own speciality. Did they help? Yes they did—thanks to Kialan again. Kialan, just this morning, had sung that song of the Adon's, and it might have been made about this very cwidder! "Unbounded truth!" Moril thought, in rising excitement. "Not a thing cramped to time and bound in place!" Neither was the cwidder, when its power was used.

He had it, then. You performed. But you did not say *Look at me*! Nor could you say, like Dagner, *This is what I think*. If Dagner's diffident way had been right, Clennen would have given the cwidder to Dagner. No. You had to stand up and come straight out with it. This is *true*, you had to say. *This is the truth.* And, though I may not get it over very well, it just *is*. And it was horribly difficult to do.

Moril blinked a little, nerving himself up. The fourth group of new recruits was shuffling its way through the valley, and Tholian was coming back again. With him were the same hearthmen who had been with him by the lake. They all had the same unpleasant look of purpose too. When they reached Kialan, Tholian jabbed at him with the toe of his boot. Kialan flopped.

"Bring him round," he said. "He's going to write me a letter presently." Then he looked across at Brid and Moril, and his eyes were like an owl's caught in a strong light at night. They knew he had no intention of sending them back to Markind.

"Moril," Brid said humbly, "do you think you can do anything?"

Moril scrambled stiffly to his feet, carefully not bumping the cwidder. "I'm going to try," he said, and began to play.

He started with a little sequence of chords, repeated over and over, in a rocking rhythm. He had to start slowly, while he found the thought the cwidder would respond to. He was terrified that Tholian would realise what he was trying to do and stop him, but, though all the men round Kialan glanced irritably at Moril, they obviously had no idea that he was doing anything important. Moril's fear faded. "Not all of you are bad," he told them through the cwidder. "Some are just afraid, others are not good, and you are doing wrong." Over and over, he told it.

And, to his relief, the cwidder began to hum under his hands. He had got it right. Moril could feel the power gather in it and then, slowly, go humming out over Tholian and his men, right off down the valley, and turn the corner to the part out of sight. The movements of everyone he could see grew slack and a little aimless, and Tholian yawned. Moril thrummed on. He would have rejoiced, except that he knew he was going to have to bring the lowest string in soon, and he was afraid of it. If its power ate into his own head this time, that was the end of his plan. Cautiously he struck it. *Sleep*, it sang, heavily sweet, off down the valley, following the humming path of the power he had already built up. *Sleep*. Tholian's head turned slowly and he looked at Moril, mistily puzzled. Moril himself was wide awake. He knew it was all right. He had been caught in the power before because he had simply been thinking *No, no, no!* without meaning anything else. Now he meant *Sleep, all you out there*.

Tholian seemed to understand what Moril was doing. He came slowly towards Moril, lurching as if he was very tired. "Break that blessed thing!" he said. His voice was slurred, but he was fighting the cwidder's power for all he was worth.

Quickly, Moril passed into a proper tune, a lullaby.

> *Go back to the time*
> *When your feelings were blind,*
> *When they rocked you and sang*
> *Go to sleep.*

If Moril had thought about it, he would have

realised he was in fact making up something new. But he did not notice, because all he wanted to do was to put Tholian to sleep. The lullaby was like a gust of power. It held Tholian to the spot. Tholian knew what was happening, but he was helpless. Moril played the tune again, louder, and took pleasure in holding Tholian in place while the tune swept beyond him, out into the valley.

Tholian rubbed his eyes and tried to take a grip on himself. Beyond him, the men round Kialan yawned and the marching and cursing in the valley faded away. The air was clear for the full force of the song, and Moril gave it them. *Go to sleep.* It went down the valley in slow waves, washing first over Tholian, then on and out. Tholian's eyelids drooped his knees bent and he dropped forward on to the trampled ground with his head in his arms. There he made one final movement of resistance and fell asleep. After him, the other people dropped down too, back and back into the valley. Horses stood still and men keeled over beside them and lay sleeping. Beside Moril, Brid fell sideways and slept curled up as if she was still kneeling. That was a pity, but Moril did not see how he could have excluded her. He played on, sending out wave after wave of sleep-song, until the valley seemed thick with it, and he could almost see it hanging in the air and pulsing gently. Under it, every soul was dead to the world.

At last, a little apprehensively, Moril left the cwidder still humming, hoping like that to make the power last, and went through the heavy, silent air to Kialan. He was still tied up. Tholian's friends had not untied him, though they had been about to. Moril went back through the humming silence and fetched the knife out of Brid's boot. "Thanks," he whispered, and he thought Brid stirred a little. With the knife he hacked through rope after tough rope, until Kialan rolled loose on the grass. He was still unconscious.

Moril bent down and shook him. "Kialan!" he said.

Kialan came round as he heard his name. Moril was almost sorry, because Kialan's face was suddenly full of pain and misery.

"It's all right," Moril whispered. "Everyone's asleep. Quick. I don't know how long it'll last."

Kialan climbed to his feet. He was very stiff and winced with every movement. He stared at Tholian, lying on the earth with his head in his arms, at Brid, and out at the silent, humming valley, full of a sleeping army. "Ye gods!" he said. "Was that the cwidder?"

"Yes," said Moril. "Quick." He ran back to Brid and shook her. Brid rolled about, but she did not wake.

Kialan came limping after him. "Suppose you leave her asleep?" he suggested. "Then when she wakes up, you'll know it's worn off."

Moril saw that was an excellent idea. The thing about Kialan, he thought as he raced for the cart, was that he had brains. Olob was dozing too, which was more serious. Moril snapped his fingers under his nose. "*Olob*! Barangarolob!" And Olob shook his head and looked at Moril wonderingly. Moril untied Olob and brought him towards Brid at a run, much though Olob objected to going near even sleeping enemies. As he hauled on the bridle, he thought how queer the valley looked with everyone in it lying asleep except for the lonely upright figure of Kialan. He dragged Olob up to Brid and opened the tailgate of the cart to make it easier to get her in. Then he gently put the cwidder back in its rack. It was still vibrating faintly.

"Throw the winejar out," said Kialan. "Let's make the cart as light as we can."

Moril heaved out the great jar. It landed with a sploshy thump that ought to have woken the dead, but Brid, who was nearest, did not stir.

Kialan laughed. "Present for Tholian. Information he knows and money he doesn't want. He can drink our health."

Moril gave a muffled giggle at the idea, but he did not speak. He had a feeling that the one thing most likely to wake the sleepers was his voice. He climbed into the cart and threw out most of Dagner's purchases: candles, flour, lentils and the remains of the rhubarb.

"Oh, he'll love those!" panted Kialan. Though he was still very stiff, he managed to lift the head and shoulders of Brid and heave the upper half of her into the cart. Moril took her shoulders and dragged her right in, where she settled with a little sigh. Kialan climbed in beside her. Moril latched the tailgate and got on to the driving seat.

"Now, Olob," he whispered. "Run. Run for your life."

Olob tossed his head and set off. He did not exactly run, but he took the cart briskly across the trampled earth to the road by which they had entered the valley. Moril looked over his shoulder as they went under the trees. Tholian was lying beside their heap of provisions. Beyond him, Moril thought he could see a faint haze vibrating quietly over the whole valley. The cwidder's power still held.

"What about those soldiers by the trestle?" Kialan said, as Olob clattered down the steep road.

"I don't know," Moril said anxiously. He had no idea how far the cwidder's power spread, and the trestle had been behind him as he played. When they came to the main road, Moril held his breath and Kialan craned sideways to get a sight of the trestle.

Those soldiers were asleep too. Most of them were sprawled in the road, pigeon breastplates upwards, snoring. One was asleep with his arms on the trestle, in a most uncomfortable position. Kialan gave a wild little laugh. "He'll be stiff when he wakes up!"

Chapter XII

It was a short, steep climb up the last of the hill. Then they came out on to the green spread of the last Upland. They could see Mark Wood in the distance, gay green and bronzed by the afternoon sun, and beyond it, looking deceptively near, the grey bulk of the Northern mountains.

"Now you *must* run, Olob," said Moril.

Olob ran. It could not be called a gallop—Moril had never known Olob to gallop in his life—but he ran, and ran as fast as Moril had ever seen him go. Behind him the lightened cart wove from side to side and bounded in the ruts of the road. Kialan wedged his feet against the side of the cart and tried to hold Brid in one place, but they nevertheless pitched and rolled and bounced until it was a marvel Brid did not wake up. But Brid slept on, stirring once or twice when she hit the side of the cart, but never coming out of her deep sleep. Moril began to hope that it would last until they reached Mark Wood. Once they were there, they could hide the cart among the trees, with a good chance of escaping Tholian.

"How did you work it?" Kialan called jerkily above the rilling of wheels and banging of hooves. "The sleep."

Moril could not explain, any more than Dagner could explain how he made songs. "By thinking," he said. "You said a lot of things that helped me."

They jounced and battered another half mile. "I had a weird dream," Kialan called, "while I was tied up. I dreamt—wow, what a bump!—I dreamt you took me along to your father's grave, by the lake, and opened that board I carved, just as if it was a door. Then you said, 'Do you mind getting in here for a while? I'll call you when it's safe to come out.' And—I say, what happens if we lose a wheel?—and I went in and went to sleep. What do you think of that?"

"I don't know," said Moril. "I might have done. There's no one behind, is there?"

There was no one, though they could hardly believe it. The wide Upland seemed empty. They rattled, wagging this way and that, through a village, and that seemed asleep too. Olob pounded on, blowing now, and Brid still slept. The sun sank and Mark Wood was nearer. Twilight seemed to come from the trees and soak into the green landscape around them. Big clouds were building up beyond the mountains. The sunset shot them with fierce pink and lakes of moist yellow.

"You know," jerked Kialan, "when I thought— in the valley—that we weren't going to get away this time, I wanted to apologise. I was pretty awful when I first came into the cart—wasn't I?"

"We were too," Moril called over his shoulder. "We didn't know what had been happening to you. Was it horrible in Holand?"

There was a bouncing, battering pause. "Ghastly," said Kialan. "But it wasn't only that. I didn't

165

understand. I thought you were all—beggars or something, and I thought—oh, of fleas and ignorance and so on for the whole way North. And I was fed up."

Moril laughed. "You looked it."

They reached the verge of Mark Wood almost as the sun set. Olob had not run so far for years. Moril could see steam rising off him in the thickening twilight. His sides were heaving under the scarlet harness, and there were flecks of foam along him. The road went upwards into the trees, under a sloping cliff, and, though it was not a steep rise, Olob slowed down.

"I'll have to let him walk," Moril said, acutely sorry for him. "He's had enough."

So Olob fell to a weary plod, and everything suddenly seemed ten times more peaceful. They could hear birds cawing and calling in the great beech trees above.

"Good gracious!" said Brid, sitting up. "Where are we? Why do I feel so bruised?"

Moril knew it was bound to happen, but he wished it had been further into the wood and not just when Olob was tired out. They explained to Brid. She was rather indignant.

"Using me as a kind of sleep-measure! I like that!"

"It was a jolly good idea," said Kialan, "though I says it as shouldn't."

But Brid had realised that Tholian was probably after them by now and changed to being as nervous as a cat. She turned her head back over her shoulder and implored Moril to get in among the trees quickly. Moril looked over his shoulder too. Between the tree trunks, he could see the darkening green of the Upland and a long stretch of the road. It was empty.

"I will when we get to the top of this hill. Olob's tired."

The dark gathered quickly under the trees, but it was still light enough to see. Brid squawked faintly. There were people among the trees on horses, coming slowly down the hill on the cliff side. But Olob gave no sign of alarm. Moril trusted Olob and kept on the road, in spite of Brid's imploring whispers. All the same, it was rather frightening the way that the horsemen, as soon as they saw the cart, turned towards it and increased their pace. They came fairly thudding down on them.

There were three of them. They drew up beside the cart, and Olob stopped walking. Kialan stood up and stared at the foremost rider, and the rider stared back.

"You blinking idiot! What did you have to come South for?" Kialan said, and burst into tears.

Somehow, though they would never have dreamt of addressing Clennen as a blinking idiot, Brid and Moril had no doubt that the rider was Keril. They watched Kialan jump awkwardly down, and the man dismount and hug him, and they were sure of it.

"Konian—they *hanged* him!" Kialan said.

"I know. We heard from a fisherman," said Keril. "It was you I came for. I was hoping Clennen might know—where *is* Clennen?" he asked.

"He's dead," said Brid, and began to cry too.

Moril sat on the driving-seat and felt tears trickling down his face. As far as he knew, he was crying for the whole situation, because he was on his own now, and always would be.

"There's an army," said Kialan. "Tholian's gathered an army to attack the North. In a valley over there. They're probably after us now."

Keril exchanged glances with the two other riders. "We've a small force in the wood. How big is this army?"

"Pretty big," Moril said, sniffing. "There were five hundred men, divided into three troops, and a hundred horsemen in the part of the valley we saw. But that was probably only a quarter of it."

"How do you know?" said Kialan. "Did you count?"

"No. I just know," said Moril. "And recruits came in four batches, while we were there, twenty-three in the first, and thirty-two in—"

"Too many for us, in fact," said Keril. "Thanks, lad. Let's get back to our camp and get fortified."

The Northerners' camp was along the cliff, chosen with an eye to defence. When tired Olob dragged the cart up to it, there was already a bustle of preparation. The campfires were being put out and the two provision waggons dragged across the only place where it could be reached from the wood. These preparations should have made Moril feel alarmed, but in fact he felt safer and happier than he had been for days. He could see by the light of the few lanterns that the mere fifty or so men bustling about had, many of them, the same dark-fair colouring as Kialan. Moril remembered now that it was something you only saw in the North. Keril was the odd man out, because he was dark, though his nose was the same shape as Kialan's.

They were taken into a tent, where they had the best meal they had had since Markind. While they were eating, Moril gathered that the Earl had been camping here for two days. The night before, he had ridden south almost to Neathdale in hopes of meeting Clennen and hearing news of Kialan, and he had been meaning to do the same that night too. It was Henda's message offering to ransom Kialan that had brought him south. Up till then, everyone in Hannart had supposed that Kialan had been hanged too.

In a tired and muddled way, they told their part, as far as Dagner's arrest. Keril, who had been sad rather than astonished at Clennen's death and not at all surprised to hear of Lenina returning to Markind, broke in angrily when he heard of Dagner. They felt sure he was thinking of Konian too, when he said, "Fancy hanging a boy that age! I wish I could *do* something—er, Moril—is that your name?"

"Not really," said Kialan. "His name's Osfameron. And Brid's Manaliabrid."

Keril forgot his anger and threw back his head and laughed.

"What's so funny?" said Brid. She was sensitive about their names.

"Well—history repeating itself, I suppose," said Keril. "Kialan's the Adon, you see."

"No he isn't," said Moril. "The Adon lived two hundred years ago. Kialan told me."

"But the heir of Hannart is always called the Adon," Keril explained, and was sad, thinking of Konian.

Moril and Kialan looked at one another by the light of the carefully-shaded lantern. Moril was thoroughly put out. If Kialan was the Adon, then he had been living the life of his dearest imaginings for nearly a month without realising it. It had not seemed like that at all. Yet, thinking of the weird dream Kialan had told him of, he suspected that it might have been history repeating itself indeed. "Why didn't you tell me?" he said.

"I didn't sort of think," said Kialan. "I was just me, trying to get home." He was thinking about his dream too. He nodded towards his father. "Tell him about the cwidder."

Moril told Keril how he put Tholian and his army to sleep. Keril marvelled a little, and he asked Kialan to confirm it, but he took it, on the whole, in the same matter-of-course way that Kialan did. "May I see the cwidder?" he said.

Moril felt his way out of the tent to the cart and came back with the cwidder. Keril took it and held it under the light of the lantern. He ran his fingers down the inlay, over the strange patterns. "Yes, this *is* the one," he said. "I used to think Clennen was boasting when he said it was Osfameron's, but I wasn't much of a hand at the old writing in those days." His square, practical-looking finger pointed to a line of swirls and dots made of slivers of mother-of-pearl. "Here it says *I sing for Osfameron* and here—" his finger moved to another line of signs—"it says *I move in more than one world.*" He smiled at Moril and handed the cwidder back. "Be careful of it."

Moril fell asleep that night hugging the cwidder, and as far removed as he could from Kialan's knees and elbows. They were a little crowded because Keril had given up his own tent to Brid. Moril had meant to do some more thinking, but he was far too tired. He awoke at dawn, because somebody came to talk to Keril, very annoyed with himself. For he was sure that, by reading the strange writing, Keril had really told him how to use the cwidder as Osfameron had used it.

There was no time for thinking for a while. The man had come to tell Keril that a troop of riders had gone by on the road during the night, and that the same troop had just come galloping back, probably on their way to report to Tholian. Both times they had been going too fast to notice the camp.

It was clear the riders had been looking for the cart. Tholian must have assumed that Moril, Brid and Kialan were driving north as fast as they could. Since the riders had not found them, Keril knew Tholian would think Kialan had already reached the North, and his news with him. "And if I were Tholian," he said, "I'd be on the march now, before the North can be ready for war. We'd better hurry."

They broke camp and went. The cart went too, with a strange youthful horse between the shafts, for more speed. Olob looked so disconsolate that Brid said she would ride him. "He'll let me," she said, "if no one puts a saddle on him. I hate him to feel neglected." So she rode Olob bareback with her boots on—for, after all, she was in company with an earl—and Olob did not seem to object. He was just rather slow. Brid had some difficulty keeping up with the cart, where Moril sat with his cwidder, thinking. The cart was being driven by a large slow-spoken Northerner called Egil, and Kialan had borrowed Egil's horse.

"You know," Brid said to Moril, "I do wish Kialan hadn't turned out to be the Adon. I feel embarrassed about liking him."

Moril was very busy thinking, but he chuckled at this. "You'll get used to it."

"You're *hopeless*!" said Brid, not as angry as she meant to be.

Kialan turning out to be the Adon was important to Moril's thoughts too. It was one of three things he kept trying to put together in his mind. The other two were what the writing said on the cwidder and his own discovery about the way you had to tell the truth with it. He thought it was odd how easily one got used to new ideas. What had seemed an entirely new thing yesterday was an old idea today, which he could use to take him on somewhere else. He went on trying to put ideas together while the band of Northerners hurried through Mark Wood.

They were not taking the road because Keril dared not risk being seen. There were clearings and villages all along the road and probably enough people in them to hold the small number of Northerners up until Tholian came to wipe them out. So they worked their way north through the trees. It was easy enough for the riders, but heavy going for the cart and the waggons. And everybody was worried about the final stretch, where they would have to come out of the trees in order to get to Flennpass. Once they were in the pass, they would be safe. It was guarded by Fort Flenn, which was the southernmost fort of the North.

Night came before they were out of the wood. Keril was anxious at their slow progress, but they had been travelling all day and they were tired. They had to risk camping for the night. After supper, round a carefully shaded campfire, they told Keril their doings in more detail. Kialan said things which confirmed Moril's feeling that his time in Holand had been more horrible than they had realised. Keril became so angry and sad that Kialan changed the subject and talked about the winejar.

"I regret leaving Tholian all that gold," he said. "He can have the rhubarb with pleasure, and the papers, but we should have taken the money out."

"Set your mind at rest," said Brid. "I did. I put it in the money-locker."

Everyone laughed. Brid wanted indignantly to know what they took her for, leaving a sum like that in a winejar.

"But I wish I knew whose it was, and where Father got it from," she said.

"I think," said Keril, "that it was probably the remains of what I gave him for expenses. I gave him a hundred gold every year in Dropwater. No," he said, when Brid offered to give it back. "Keep it. You deserve it. You can use it as pocket money when you're living in Hannart."

In this way, they gathered that Keril intended them to live with him in Hannart.

"That's frightfully nice of you," Brid said awkwardly. "Because I don't know what else we'd do, do you, Moril?"

"It's the least I can do," said Keril. "I owe Clennen a great deal. If it hadn't been for him, we'd have had no news from the South worth having." Then he told them things about Clennen they had not known before. Keril had met Clennen in the South in the days when he was still only the Adon, and they had both helped in the uprising there. But Keril's father died and he had to go North. Clennen stayed in the South, until soon after he met Lenina. Then, what with old Tholian's fury and the failure of the uprising, Clennen found the South too hot to hold him. He went to Hannart and became singer to the court. Dagner, Brid and Moril had all been born in Hannart. It had been Clennen's idea to go south again, when they heard reports of what was going on. The Porter had been his idea too. But Keril had thought of staging the quarrel so that no one would suspect Clennen was Hannart's agent.

Moril sat staring into the fire, dreaming of Hannart.

"What is it, Moril?" Kialan said jokingly. "Dreams coming true?"

Moril looked up and grinned. He did not say anything, but he went to sleep sure that Kialan had just told him the way the cwidder really worked.

He thought it out as he rode in the cart next day. It came to him first as a memory. It had rained in Crady, so Clennen had told one of the stories of the Adon indoors, and Moril had looked up to see Kialan in the audience. He had been annoyed, because he thought of Kialan as part of dreary, everyday life, and he had felt as if he had a foot in two worlds which were spinning apart from one another. Yet Kialan was the Adon—or *an* Adon—all the time. And the cwidder itself said *I move in more than one world.*

It came on to rain just then, though not as heavily as it had rained in Crady. Moril smiled and lifted his face into the wet. They were nearly in the North, and it rained a lot there. His smile became rather rueful as he realised that, in none of his dreams of Hannart or hazy imaginings of the cart on green roads, had he ever thought of it raining. The cwidder had made a muzzy sound. And that was the point. That kind of dream was not true. There were true dreams, but they had to be part of life as well, just as life, to be good, had to embody dreams, or a good song had to have an idea to it. The Adon's song Kialan had sung had been saying that. But Osfameron's song had gone one further and talked of the other worlds the cwidder moved in.

Moril thought of the way life and dreams had met for him, willy-nilly, on this journey. But he knew they met in him naturally too, when he could be miles away, thinking, and yet count all the soldiers in that valley, or every beech tree they were passing at the moment. He saw that Clennen had not got it quite right. He had been too practical to see. The important thing was that Moril *was* in two halves. Provided he knew what was true in both, he could use the cwidder as it should be used. He could send ideas through it, into reality.

About mid-morning, they came to the end of Mark Wood. Moril looked past Egil's broad back at the mountains at last, vividly close, and the deep V in them that was Flennpass. The rain had stopped, but the clouds over the mountains were heavy with more. It was a grey, threatening scene. Flenn Fort was out of sight, behind a sharp peak, since it was at the North end of the pass, but Moril could see the South's answer to it. The wood had been cleared for a mile or so in front of the pass, so that no one could go in or out of it unseen. He looked at the mountains across a desolation of tree-stumps, charred from frequent burning, with new bright green bushes and saplings springing up between, because it had not yet been cleared this year.

The Northerners stopped at the edge of the trees. Moril did not at first know why.

"The Lord of Mark, I think," Keril said to his captain. "Tholian must have set him to watch for the cart."

Moril leant round Egil and his stomach fluttered at the number of the horsemen drawn up across the pass in the distance. They were clearly Southerners, and in war-gear, and there were at least twice as many of them as there were Northerners in Keril's band.

"He can't be expecting us," said the captain. "I'll take an oath no one saw us come through. It'll give him a fair old shock when we ride out at him."

"I know," said Keril, "but I'd be more comfortable if we were twice the number."

"Oh come!" said someone else, laughing. "One Northerner's worth ten Southerners. Any day."

Moril thought for a moment. Yes. Everyone believed that. None of the band was particularly worried, and even Brid was looking confidently at Keril, sure they would get past the Lord of Mark without trouble. Northerners were famous fighters. But Keril was evidently thinking it was more important to get through to the North than to get courageously killed on the way.

"Would you like there to seem more of us?" Moril called over to him. "I think I can do it."

Keril made a bit of a face. "I only wish you could."

"I bet he can," said Kialan.

Moril slung the cwidder round his neck and began to play the *Eighth March*. It was never played in the South, for obvious reasons. But, as Clennen often said, it went to such a brisk time that only the North thought of it as a march.

> *We are the men of the North, the North,*
> *And I'll tell you how much we're worth, we're*
>   *worth—*
> *One man is as good as ten Southern men*
> *And each of us marches as ten.*

For a moment, until the cwidder began to hum, Moril was afraid he had got it wrong after all. But the hum increased and became almost like a light-hearted whistling, and the wood was suddenly full of men, horses and waggons. Some of the Northerners cried out in alarm.

Kialan burst out laughing. "Oh, well done, Moril! Only nine more pink carts are a bit much!"

Moril glanced from side to side and could not help laughing. There were indeed nine more pink carts. One of them had a tree apparently growing through it. And a false Moril sat in each playing an illusory cwidder. What he had done was to reflect their own band nine times over, just as the song said. After all, it was an illusion that one Northman was worth ten Southerners. And the riders and waggons were exactly that, like reflections in a mirror, the Northmen realised. People began to laugh and wave at their own reflections. Consequently, the false nine-tenths waved and laughed also.

Keril laughed with the rest. "Keep playing, Moril. Off we go."

Moril played on gaily, and they moved out from among the trees, the real and the false men together.

They rode through the bushes and stumps under a stormy sky, towards the road, and the real men had to go round saplings and the larger stumps, but Moril's illusions went straight through everything in their path. When they reached the road, there was a good deal of confusion and much laughter. The Northmen tried to get out of the way of their own shadows, until they grasped that there were four reflections on the left and five to the right, and that the fifth band from the left was the real one, entitled to use the road. Once they had sorted that out, they trotted on in fine style, many of them singing the *Eighth March* as Moril played. And, on either side, the nine repetitions went straight through the landscape, pink carts through bushes and horses through saplings.

Moril sat in the midmost pink cart beaming with elation. It was the most splendid proof that he had done his thinking right. The whistling hum of the cwidder in his hands, calling the strange army into being, took on an extra note, like a sort of purring, as it reflected Moril's pleasure and amusement. Behind him, Brid and Kialan thought it one of the funniest things they had seen. They thought it even funnier when Olob sensed enemies near and began prancing about, setting the nine other Olobs prancing too, and the nine other Kialans grabbing at his bridle to help Brid control him.

By the pass, the Lord of Mark's force drew uneasily together, seeing five hundred apparent Northmen riding merrily towards them. As Keril's band drew nearer, they could see the enemies' uneasiness mounting. Ordinary Northerners maybe they could face. But what was to be done with enemies who went straight through small trees and seemed none the worse for it? When they were near enough to distinguish faces, and only a hundred yards from the camp the Lord of Mark had set up to the right of the road, a group of the Southerners panicked and had to be brought back by some others. Moril could see a man who must be the Lord of Mark riding up and down imploring his men to keep calm. He laughed. Then two shadow waggons and a pink cart went right through the camp without disturbing so much as guyrope. A number of the Southerners wailed with terror. Moril thought, Why not? and threw in the lowest string. *Run*! it boomed beneath the gay tune.

The Lord of Mark broke and ran, and his men with him. They galloped frantically away to right and left along the mountains and vanished in the bushes, leaving Flennpass open. A roar of laughter went up from Keril's band.

Brid's voice cut through it. "Moril! *Look*!"

Moril glanced back. Huge numbers of horsemen were on the dark edge of Mark Wood, and more were among the trees. The horses' legs were all moving steadily, but they were too far away for sound to carry, and the riders seemed to glimmer along as if they were an illusion too. Only they were no such thing. They were the forefront of Tholian's army.

Chapter XIII

Moril gave the alarm with a sweep of his hand on the cwidder. Though Keril also looked over his shoulder, it was only to confirm what the cwidder said. In that same moment, they were all going hell for leather for Flennpass and Flenn Fort at the other end of it. The ghostly nine-tenths had gone as if they had never been. Moril knew there was no time for illusions. As the cart bucked and wove along, he hung on to the side and looked back.

Tholian's army was coming at a steady speed across the cleared stretch. If anyone saw the cart, or the sudden decrease in the size of their band, there was no sign of it. The host of horsemen simply came onward. It might be pursuing Keril, but it looked more as if their band would be merely the first incident in the invasion. Tholian had no need to hurry, since the North was unprepared. Olob knew the army was behind and Brid could not control him. Kialan had taken the reins and was dragging him along with Egil's horse. Moril thought this might well make Olob worse. Olob had never really accepted Kialan. But there was nothing Moril could do.

They swept into the pass with a gathering thunder of hooves. It held a good road between cliff-like walls, which narrowed at the Northern end. They had to string out as they went, with the cart and the waggons bouncing in the rear. Egil and the other drivers were using their whips. Brid was smacking Olob. Moril thought they would just make it to the fort, though it would be a close thing —and it seemed closer every second. The army behind had no waggons with the vanguard to slow them down. They were catching up steadily. As Keril's troop came to the narrowest part of the pass, where the fort stood chunkily above on the skyline, Moril looked round to see the first line of Tholian's cavalry coming into the wide end of the pass, and multitudes of others milling behind.

Keril had reached the fort, when Moril looked back, and was shouting to the people inside. There was a moment's delay. But the defenders must have seen all that happened. A sudden black space appeared where the great gate had been, and some of the Northmen rode into it. The space between the cliffs was filled with noise, the huge drumming of a mass of hooves, and some sharper sounds. Moril thought the fort was firing on the enemy.

Things began to fall around the cart and bounce off the waggons. They were not from the fort, but from the advancing army. Moril could do nothing but hope. It was long-range, and he thought it must be difficult to fire from a cantering horse. But to Olob, struggling against Kialan's impatient hand on his bridle, it was the last straw. In his terror, he turned clean round, dragging Kialan and Egil's horse with him. Brid lurched and hung on to his mane. A number of the Northmen saw what was happening and turned back to help. And the narrow end of the pass at once became a dangerous bottle-neck, full of riders trying to go two ways at once. Egil roared out a curse and pulled the cart up. Moril jumped down, with the cwidder slung across his shoulders, and ran towards Olob.

"Let him go!" he shouted to Kialan. "Olob, stop it!"

Luckily, Kialan had the sense to let go. For, as Moril ran up, Olob reared, frightened out of his wits. There were just too many enemies for him. Moril had to dodge his lashing front hooves, and Brid slid helplessly down his back, over his tail and on to the ground. And, as Olob stood high above them, screaming and slashing, an unlucky bullet took him clean through the head. His great brown body came down between Moril and Brid with the force of a falling oak. He was dead before he hit the ground.

They stared at one another over the huge corpse.

"Olob now," said Brid.

"Right!" said Moril. "That does it!"

Keril's captain had been sorting out the bottle-neck. Now he galloped up and held down his hand to Brid. "Catch hold, lass! Up you come!" Brid caught hold and scrambled up behind him.

Kialan shouted to Moril and held down a hand to him, but Moril did not attend. He raced to the cliff at the side of the pass and climbed it like a maniac with the cwidder bumping and booming on his back. He was at the top in ten seconds—how, he never knew. Heaving deep breaths, he went scrambling along the cliff-edge until he had a view down into the pass. He saw Kialan, not very far below him, at the gate of the fort, waving and shouting something. He seemed to mean there was a door in the fort at the top of the cliff. Then he went into the fort and the gate shut.

But Moril, now he knew the Northmen were in the fort, was not interested in the door. He looked southward along the pass. It was packed with Tholian's horsemen more than halfway along. They were going more slowly now, because of the narrower space, and, beyond the wide end of the pass, as far as he could see, there were more riders coming. It was truly an invasion.

Moril stood up and slung the cwidder in front of him. He felt a spatter of rain. There looked to be a storm coming, which was all to the good. For a second, he gazed up at the heavy bruise-like clouds, feeling a little awed. He thought anyone would who was about to use the cwidder as Osfameron had used it.

Then he looked down into the pass where Olob's body lay in the middle of the road. The nearest riders were not so far from it now. He struck one sharp, rolling chord, and the power in the cwidder swelled with it. There was no humming, but he could feel the power. "You're not coming North," he said to the jostling riders. "And this is why." He struck two more chords. The power almost choked him. The answer was a great dagger of lightning, green and perilous, lancing down over the cliffs. A peal of thunder followed, and Moril led it on, pealing the lowest note of the cwidder, so that the power in it could grow. When it stopped, he spoke, in the way the singers spoke an incantation. He said:

Kialan and Konian were caught in a storm.

> The one you hanged in Holand had not harmed
>   anyone,
> Nor had Kialan when you caught him. This is
>   for Konian first.

He struck another chord, followed by a swinging, hanging, frantic phrase, and felt the power in the cwidder grow again. Then he said:

> Unlucky Clennen lies by a lake in Markind,
> The singer you stabbed on suspicion only
> And prevented him performing. This is for the
>   Porter Clennen.

He struck a sharp chord and a rolling one. The first horsemen were now right beneath him. They did not pause when they came to Olob, but trampled over him and on. Moril saw, but he looked beyond them, to the centre of the pass. Tholian was there, jostled on either side by his favourite friends. Moril waited, quite confident and implacable, and let them come on while the power in the cwidder grew yet again. Then he spoke his last stave:

> There was no mercy shown by the magistrate in
>   Neathdale
> To Dastgandlen Handagner. There was death in
>   the South
> And weeping in the Uplands. Now war comes
>   North,
> And all through Tholian. This is for Tholian.

He struck the cwidder again, and again, and yet a third time, vengefully. The power grew enormous, until it possessed Moril, the sky, the clouds, and the entire pass. Then, as Moril had known they would, the hills began to walk.

They started mildly and slowly, as if the mountains on either side of the pass were shrugging their shoulders. But, in a second or so, the shrugging was a deep rhythmic jigging. The tops of the cliffs bent and marched, regularly inwards and downwards, walking, piling, inescapably trudging together to fill the pass. The thunder pealed and was drowned in the grinding of ton after ton of rock, moving and jogging inwards. Almost lost in the greater din was the lesser screaming of men and horses. At the far end of the pass, Moril could see riders swirling and struggling to get back or get out. But leisurely, sleepily, rhythmically, the mountains were filling the centre. The cliff Moril was on marched with the rest, downwards and forwards. Moril leant backwards to keep his balance and let it take him, until he was standing at the head of a heap of jumbled rocks, almost over the place where Olob had been shot. The rocks were piled into the rift, choking it so that it was no longer a pass.

Moril did not spend long looking, because the rain came down, and the torn surfaces of the rocks were black with it. But he knew, as he turned round to keep the cwidder from the worst of the wet and stripped off his coat to cover it, that Tholian was underneath somewhere and Barangarolob had plenty of company. He looked across to see that the fort was safe, as he had intended. It was there, standing on a steep-sided block of steady rock, and Keril was picking his way over the ruin of the cliff towards him.

"I've just done something really horrible," Moril said to him. "Haven't I?"

Keril jumped from one rock to another, and then

on to the one where Moril stood. "I don't think we had much chance of holding the pass otherwise," he said.

"You don't understand," said Moril. "I did it because of Olob." He leant against Keril and burst into tears. Keril took off his own coat, wrapped it round Moril, and led him quietly back over the rocks to the fort.

They left the fort the following day, after a big force of men from the North Dales arrived there to make sure the Southerners did not attempt to attack over the fallen rocks. Moril did not see as much of the journey to Hannart as he would have liked. He was exhausted, and spent most of the time asleep in one of the waggons. Every so often he woke to find they were on a green road, or in a wood where the trees were still only budding in the later spring of the North, and went to sleep happy. He was awake to see the Falls at Dropwater, which he would not have missed for worlds. And by the time they reached Hannart he had come to himself again.

He was disappointed, but not really surprised, to find Hannart a city far larger than Neathdale, in the centre of a big valley. Flags were flying in honour of their arrival. There were crowds of people carrying flags or flowers. Hannart was full of flowers, in fields, in gardens, on trees, and growing wild, thick as the grass, on the steep sides of the mountains. Moril could smell them as soon as they entered the valley. At the end of the valley was a great tall thing, like a castle four times life-size, picked out in gold and blue and green.

Moril stared at it. "Whatever is that?"

"That's the steam organ," said Kialan. "Haven't you heard about it? They'll probably play it tonight. It makes the most splendid noise."

"I wish someone had told me," said Moril.

There was a feast that night, in their honour, and, as Kialan had thought, the steam organ played. In a strong steamy smell of coal and oil, it thundered out well-known tunes, like a mountain singing, or the grandfather of all music, and made Brid and Moril laugh. It seemed most fitting that Hannart should own such a thing, because the place was full of music, not only then, but at all times. Cowbells clinked in the steep meadows. Women called the cows home in a kind of song, not unlike Brid's *Cow-calling* song. In the city, there were tunes for crying everything that was on sale and for telling the hours of the watch. There was singing and dancing somewhere almost every night. The saying was that you could tell someone came from Hannart because whatever they did they sang, and if they did not sing they whistled.

Keril lived right in the centre of the city, in a house twice the size of Ganner's. Unlike Ganner's house, it was always open. The cheerful people of Hannart seemed to use its front courtyard as another part of the main square. There was always someone there, gossiping or selling something, and, if anything unusual happened, they came on into the rest of the house to tell Keril about it. Since there were also large numbers of people who actually lived in the house, Moril found it almost impossible to sort out who came from where.

Brid loved it. She had never been happier in her life. "I often remembered it, but I didn't think it was real!" she was fond of saying.

Moril enjoyed it too. He liked the liveliness, the carelessness, and the way people rushed up to Keril and said what they pleased. He could not imagine anyone doing that in the South. Moril liked Keril. He liked Halida, Kialan's mother. He enjoyed being with Kialan, and he loved the perpetual music. But he was too hot in the city and far too hot in the house. He kept having to go out on the hillsides. At night, it was worse, and he slept in one of the gardens when he could. When Halida realised this, she gave him a room on the ground floor, opening on one of the gardens. Moril was grateful, but he hardly went into the room, and he only slept there if it was raining.

Brid and Kialan consulted about it and went to see what Keril thought.

"Yes," said Keril. "I'm afraid he'll be off again, one of these days. I hope not yet, though. I owe it to Clennen to see he has an education."

After that, Brid watched Moril like a hawk. Moril showed no sign of wanting to leave. He seemed perfectly happy getting the education Keril thought he should have. He spent long hours playing his cwidder with Kialan, arranging songs and trying to make new ones. He rode with Kialan and Brid, and walked on the hills with them. It was just that he was too hot indoors, and there was something at the back of his mind he did not want to think about yet.

Now Flennpass was blocked, there was very little news from the South. It was nearly a month before some fishermen brought news that Tholian had indeed been killed by the fall of rocks, and his army, most of it having been unwilling anyway, had packed up and gone home. Some time after that, a trader arrived to say that things had gone very quiet in the South. Yes, he said, when Keril questioned him, the lords and earls were very shaken. But the cause of the quiet was the ordinary people. They did nothing, but they seemed powerful. The earls were afraid of them. They dared not even try for peace with the North, in case that stirred up a revolution.

A month later still, a cart drove into Hannart. By the black mud on its axles, it had clearly come north through the Marshes. Apart from the mud, it was gaily painted in green and gold, and trim enough. It was driven by a very pretty girl. Beside her on the driving-seat sat a dreamy-looking man with a thin face and a thin, greying beard, who smiled round at the gaiety of Hannart with a look of mild pleasure. The small gold lettering on the side of the cart said he was *HESTEFAN THE SINGER*.

The people of Hannart realised that here would be both music and more news of the South. Numbers followed the cart as it jogged through the streets and drove into the front court of the Earl's house.

"Oh look! A singer!" Brid said to Kialan.

"Do you know him?" Kialan asked Moril.

"I've heard of him," said Moril. He looked at Hestefan's mild face and dreamy eyes, and it came to him that he would probably look like that when he was older.

The cart stopped. The mottled grey horse blew,

as much as to say, "Good—that's enough for today, thank you." The canvas cover came back a little, and a third traveller rather hesitantly stood up in the cart.

"*Dagner!*" shrieked Brid, Moril and Kialan.

They rushed up and hurled themselves on him. Dagner, grinning and blushing mauve with pleasure, climbed out of the cart and was thrown against it by their onrush.

"What happened?" said Brid.

"How did you get out of prison?" said Moril.

"Ganner got me out," Dagner said, when he had got his breath back. "Ganner's a good fellow. I got to like him a lot. He did follow us, you know, but he went back to Markind when he didn't find us. Then—I don't know what you said to that old snob of a Justice, Moril, but when they had me up in front of them again, they didn't seem at all sure I was guilty and kept asking me about Ganner. So I told them he was marrying Mother, and they sent all the way to Markind to ask if it was true. It was marvellous. As soon as Ganner heard I was in prison, he came to Neathdale and raised a real stink. And while he was doing it, news came that Tholian was dead. Ganner upped and sacked the Justice, and said he was in charge now. It was marvellous! He let half the other prisoners go too. But, seeing that I really had been passing information, Mother thought I'd better go North for a while and got Hestefan to take me."

"How is Mother?" asked Moril.

"Terribly happy," said Dagner. "Runs about all the time laughing. I don't know why—she laughed when she heard Flennpass was blocked and said you and Brid must have made it to the North. She sent me with a letter for you both."

Brid and Moril snatched the letter and bent over it eagerly. It was a good long letter, all about Lenina's doings in Markind. Lenina wrote of everything from the speckled cows to the roof where Moril had walked, and reminded Brid of this and Moril of that, and sent Ganner's love—and, to Moril, it was like a letter from a distant acquaintance. He felt it might just as well have been written to the baker's boy round the corner. He was sad that he should feel like that, but he could not help it.

"What a lovely letter!" said Brid. "I shall keep it."

While they were reading it, Hestefan's pretty daughter had driven the cart away to the stables. Moril was annoyed, because he had wanted to talk to Hestefan. He dashed away to the stables, but the green cart was already standing empty in the coach-house beside their battered and faded pink one. Moril went back to the courtyard, where Dagner, delighted to see them all again, was being uncharacteristically chatty.

"Shall I tell you something really silly?" he said to Kialan, as Moril came up. "You won't believe this!"

"Try me," said Kialan.

"Well," said Dagner, "I'm the Earl of the South Dales. They won't have me," he said hastily, as Kialan burst out laughing. "Nothing will possess them to invest me. But it's true. Tholian wasn't married, and all his cousins were killed too, when Flennpass collapsed—you *must* tell me about that, by the way—and the only living heir left was me. And Moril after that. Honestly."

Moril stood silent in the crowded courtyard and left Brid and Kialan to do the exclaiming. Now he knew what it was that he had not wanted to think about. He had done that. He had worked a huge destruction and killed so many people that Dagner was now an earl. Everyone no doubt thought he had done right. He had saved the North, prevented a war, and avenged Clennen and Konian. But Moril knew he had not done right. He had done it all because Olob was killed. With the cwidder in his hands, he had behaved as if it was for Konian, for Clennen, for Dagner and for the North, but it had all been for Olob really. He was ashamed. What he had done was to cheat the cwidder. That was the worst thing. If you stood up and told the truth in the wrong way, it was not true any longer, though it might be as powerful as ever. Moril saw that he was neither old enough nor wise enough to have charge of such a potent thing as that cwidder.

That night, there was a feast in honour of Dagner, Hestefan and Fenna, Hestefan's daughter. Keril asked Hestefan to sing. Hestefan sang, old songs, new songs, and many that Moril had never heard. When he sang, you forgot it was Hestefan singing and only thought of the song. Moril was impressed. Then Hestefan told a story. It was one Moril did not know. And, while Hestefan was telling it, he found he forgot who was telling it and simply lived in the story. Moril realised he still had a lot to learn.

After that, they wanted Dagner to sing. Dagner was nervous, but surprisingly ready to perform.

"Huh!" said Brid. "He just wants to impress Fenna, that's what."

Whatever the reason, Dagner took his own cwidder, fetched for him by Kialan, tuned it, and sang the song Moril had tried to finish for him. He did it nothing like the way Moril had made it go. The new parts of the tune were quite different from Moril's, and he had changed the beginning. It now went:

> *Follow me, follow me.*
> *The blackbird sings to follow me.*
> *No one will know where we go—*
> *All that matters is we go.*

Kialan looked at Moril and made a face to show that he liked Moril's version better. Moril smiled. Everyone had to do things their own way. While Dagner went on to sing his *Colour* song, Moril slipped quietly away, fetched the old cwidder, slung it on his shoulders, and went to where Hestefan was refreshing himself with beer beside an open window. Hestefan looked as if he was too hot, just like Moril.

"Please," Moril said to him, "will you take me with you when you go?"

"Well," Hestefan said dubiously, "I was thinking of slipping off now, while nobody's noticing."

"I know you were," said Moril. "Take me too. Please."

Hestefan looked at him, a vague, dreamy look, which, Moril was positive, saw twice as much as most people's. "You're Clennen's other son, aren't you?" he said. "What's your name?"

"Tanamoril," said Moril. "I'm called Osfameron too," he added, as an inducement.

Hestefan smiled. "Very well then," he said. "Come along."